Guilty and Free

MASCOT BOOKS
an imprint of Amplify Publishing Group

www.mascotbooks.com

Guilty and Free: A Novel

For more information, please contact:
Mascot Books, an imprint of Amplify Publishing Group
620 Herndon Parkway, Suite 220
Herndon, VA 20170
info@amplifypublishing.com

Library of Congress Control Number: 2025912523

CPSIA Code: PRV0925A

ISBN-13: 979-8-89138-559-7

Printed in the United States

To all my ancestors that came before
me and to all the ancestors that will
come after me.

Thank you for my slice of life.

GUILTY AND FREE

a novel

DON ROSE

MASCOT BOOKS
an imprint of Amplify Publishing Group

CAST OF CHARACTERS

MAIN CHARACTERS

George Francis . . . . .patriarch

Gina George . . . . .Francis's deceased wife

Frank James . . . . George's son and a police detective

Carla . . . . Frank James's deceased wife

Sabrina . . . . George's daughter, married to Sam

Sam Jefferson . . . . . husband to Sabrina and fireman/paramedic

Kari . . . . Frank's daughter, married to Jason

Jason . . . . .married to Kari

Nelson . . . . Kari's son, married to Rita

Rita . . . . married to Nelson

Jacob . . . . Nelson and Rita's son who has the *gift*

Lyndsey . . Sabrina's daughter, married to Ernie Jones, paramedic

Rob . . . . .Lyndsey's son

Mary . . . . Lyndsey's daughter

Tiffany Rose . . . . Sabrina's daughter, married to Manny

Lori . . . . .Tiffany Rose's daughter

Kelsea . . . . .honorary member of the family

OTHER CHARACTERS

Michael Jacobson . . . . .detective with Frank James

Max Jefferson. . . . . .murder suspect

Mike Westwood . . . . murder victim

Liz Westwood . . . . murder suspect

Phyllis Granger . . . . murder victim

Jack Evans .murder suspect at the marina

Kaytlin . . . . Sabrina's cover name at the marina

Tony Romano . . defense lawyer at Romano, Murphy, & Erickson

Frank O'Brian . . . . banker at Taylor Central Bank

Payton Riley . . . . small-time crook/drug dealer

Carlos Lopez . . . . La Aguila (the Eagle) drug cartel

Anna Romano . .office manager at Romano, Murphy, & Erickson

Dean Wilson . . . . police detective

Ben Holloway . . . . police detective

Roberta Jones . . . . .physical therapist

Bernard Bakers . . . . .serial rapist

Ava Kaiser . . . . .insider trader

Senator Chester Booth . . . . senator

Sergio Martinez . . . . diamond dealer

Barbara Sinclair . . . . Sabrina's cover for diamonds

Rafael Sinclair . . . . Frank's cover for diamonds

Emily Carson . . . . CEO at Children's Life

Regan Staples . . . . .Emily's boyfriend

Kelly Taylor . . . . Sabrina's cover name while in Switzerland

Jackson Garwood . . . . domestic abuser

Donna Cup . . . . 10-million-dollar lottery winner

Leslie Cup . . . . Donna's daughter

Daniel Oscar Allen . . . . DOA

Peter Owens . . . . B-list celebrity

Giana . . . . world-famous model

Sissy Andrews . . . . .flight attendant

Johnny Murphy . . . . .A-list celebrity

Juan Pablo . . . . hedge fund financial consultant

Diego . . . . Bermuda cave guide

Taylor . . . . .Juan Pablo's girlfriend

Oliver Bundy . . . . bad bloodline

Bernhard Bauer . . . . bad bloodline

Riley Juarez . . . . bad bloodline

Morgan Ann Miller . . . . nurse at Kensington Hospital

Marie Jean Phillips . . . . nurse

Matt Ryan Dalton . . . . nurse

Burton Douglas . . . . marine biologist

Ivan Statin . . . . relative of Joseph Stalin

Alexi Statin . . . . relative of Joseph Stalin

Dmitri Statin . . . . relative of Joseph Stalin

Arthur Dillinger . . . . human trafficker

Kelly Barns . . . . child abductor

Diego Martinez . . . . child abductor

Gabriel . . . . angel

Bobby Ray Kenny . . . . rapist

Mario Mayfield . . . . professional criminal

Dominick Amaral . . . . math teacher, football coach

Marley Brown . . . . human trafficker/drug runner

Adio Azan . . . . leader of the DanDan Jamaican cartel

Anant Sharman . . . . CEO of the Sand Storm Company

Raj Bakshi . . . . second-in-command of the Sand Storm Company

Harald Thorson . . . . mafia head of Thorson Construction

CHAPTER 1

GEORGE FRANCIS IS DEAD.

He led the family for many years and watched the family members with the *gift* grow into something he was proud of. A family patriarch obsessed with killing just one person: someone who deserved to die. A life's passion. A passion he experienced; a lifelong dream he accomplished. He trained his whole life for this one desire, this one murder.

He had selected his victim carefully after reviewing many potential victims. This victim had stood out, and after sneaking into his house, he injected his special brown liquid into the victim's neck, which rendered his victim, Victor, helpless. Victor's mind, eyes, and sensations were fully alert, but his ability to move any muscle was gone.

George Francis strangled Victor slowly but steadily, watching his terrified eyes slowly close, his accelerated breath slow down and stop, and his racing heart go from beating wildly to not beating at all. George Francis had witnessed death up close and personal. A life's dream and passion to watch someone die at his hands. George had thought that this one killing, which he had prepared his whole life for, would be the end of his desire to kill. But he was wrong. His inner beast demanded more, so George began to look for people that seemed to have a red glow.

George could see the people who were unworthy of life, people who appeared with an aura of red, from a soft, wispy red all the way to a vibrant red. The bright red indicated the worst offenders. These are considered people not worthy of life, who have committed a crime against humanity, such as a murderer or a soulless person that takes advantage of others. A person who inflicts emotional wounds on others.

Something inside George demanded his attention. Two things, in fact. It was hard to tell them apart sometimes, but there was a violent, bloodthirsty force that George called "the monster" and a more protective force that cared for his well-being, which he called "the dark passenger." George spent a lifetime accommodating these companions.

George thought he was the only person to have this gift, as he called it. He was utterly astonished when he discovered his son, Frank James, had the same desire, the same goal, the same inner beast. George taught his son all he knew, and the two began to make rules and guidelines to follow: a code of conduct so that they would not be caught.

George Francis lived a full life and lived long enough to see the family, with the gift, expand. When the time comes, George witnesses his own death with awe, fully experiencing it. His eyes, his heart, and his breath all stopped by his own granddaughter, Sabrina. It is glorious. Sabrina has the family gift—though it's a gift that not all the family shares. With Frank's sad approval, Sabrina sends her grandfather into the next world. What is the next world? No one alive knows, but George Francis now knows. He is there.

Frank approves but is shocked by the death. He is sad to see his father die but, at the same time, thrilled. His own inner demons are excited, his dark passenger full of electricity. But, as it is happening, when he looks at the staircase behind him, he sees his daughter Kari is watching George Francis die. Kari is lying at the top of the stairs watching Sabrina, her cousin, strangle her grandfather.

Kari should be shocked, but she feels totally alive and excited to see death so close-up. She is sad to see her papa die, and her emotions are off the scale. Happy, thrilled, sad, and shocked, but with an intense joy at his death. She can't figure out her emotions, but all her life she has felt different from other kids her age. She is excited whenever death is a subject to be discussed. No one else seems to feel like her. Death is not an enemy, not a foe, but a friend. She often asks herself, *Does it scare me? No, I embrace it; I feel its power. I feel the quiet rage inside me. Am I repulsed? No, I am invigorated. I am confused.* Her dad, Frank James, runs toward her as he slams the door where Sabrina and Papa are doing a death dance. He grabs her and hugs her tight.

Frank says, "Kari, you should not have seen that. I am so sorry you saw that."

Kari says, "Dad, I saw you full of excitement. I saw you fully in the moment, and I saw joy in your face. I don't know what is going on, but Sabrina, you, and I are all excited and part of the same thing, whatever that is. I think you know. I think Sabrina knows, and I think Papa was a part of it. I am part of something, but I don't know what. But we are all in it. We are all connected. Please help me. I feel like I'm going crazy, and I have felt this for a long time. I feel a monster in me, a demon. I have a quiet rage that yearns to get out. I have been able to control it up till now, but tonight I feel movement inside me. Help me control this thing that wants to control me. Help, Dad."

Sabrina emerges from George Francis's home office. She is tense but glowing, trembling from excitement. She looks from Kari to Frank James and back again.

"Kari, I'm sorry you had to see that. Let me explain."

Kari stops Sabrina with her hand up and says, "Sabrina, I know what I saw, and both you and my dad were excited, and your emotions were off the scale. But please tell me why I see red."

Kari is bright red, as are her dad and her aunt Sabrina. Frank tells his daughter Kari, "The color in the family gives us immunity from guilt and remorse. It allows us the strength and ability to kill without conscience. It protects us. The color also points out those that we see as unworthy."

"Whatever I am involved with, I can see that you are way ahead of me," Kari says. "Please don't brush this off and patronize me, but include me in what is happening. Why is my papa George dead? Why did he have to die? What is going on? Why do I have such feelings electrifying my body? Why am I feeling something deep and dark within me, satisfied by what I witnessed? Help me."

Frank gently puts his arm around Kari and guides her toward George Francis's office and walks in. "Sabrina, join us. Lock the door."

The three are now in the room where George Francis is slumped in his desk chair, the red glow gone but the halo effect from the thrill of death still around him. They sit on the sofa with Kari sitting between them.

Her dad starts, "Kari, we have a dark passenger that resides inside us. It is in the family, but not all of us have the 'gift,' as we call it. Your grandfather never admitted that he had the gift, but Sabrina and I know different."

Sabrina adds, "We knew my dad had the dark passenger, but he had trained himself his whole life to deny the dark passenger, so he could not, would not, tell us."

Kari asks, "What is a dark passenger?"

Frank says, "We in the family have this dark side that craves murder. We each have a calling, a duty, to kill. To see the breathing slow, then stop, to see the eyes fill with terror, then shut down with death. To feel a death caused by our actions. From strangulation to guns, knives, and all sorts of methods of death. What you saw tonight was Sabrina's death dance with Papa. His time had come. With him losing your grandmother, he was not himself. He was also losing his mind slowly, but the dark passenger, the inner monster, in him would not let him have peace. It was demanding he go out and murder. He was planning to murder again to satisfy these monsters."

Sabrina continues, "Kari, some of us have the dark passenger and some have the inner beast, the inner monster. Some of us have both. The dark passenger is calculating, devious, and determined to protect us. The inner monster is emotional, terrifying, strong, unrelenting, and aggressive. We have discovered as a family that we need to fight our call of duty to eliminate people."

Frank says, "Kari, if my father had gone out now and murdered, there was a good chance he would have been caught. He was not being careful, and he was not including Sabrina or me because he knew we disapproved of the changes in him. He was having dementia issues, and his reasoning was not sound. He was not capable of committing any murder in his condition, both mentally and physically. If he did get caught, the police would look into his life, his world, and us, his family. We would all be caught. We could not explain the murders we have been involved with. Your grandfather would have brought the entire family down. That is why Sabrina took the action she did."

Kari says, "I understand, kind of. How will I know if I have the passenger and the beast?"

Frank says, "Time will tell. Currently, Sabrina, Papa, and I have been the only ones in the family who have committed murder, but we have been careful and meticulous. We could not let my father live. He knew this. He knew his time was coming. He knew we would have to act, and he was in agreement in the moments when his mind was clear. Papa was glad it was Sabrina; you could see it in his eyes. As sad as it is, it was the right decision. I am so sorry you had to find out this way."

Sabrina holds her niece's hand and says, "Papa knew his lifetime was almost finished, and he knew his killing time was finished. It scared me, but I knew I would have to send Papa into the next world."

Kari replies, "I understand what you are saying, but I don't think I could act on my desire. I could not have killed my papa."

Sabrina says, "Educating you on our ways may change your mind. How long have you known you are different?"

"I have always known that I am not the same as other girls. I have always known I had something inside of me that craved death. I thought I was going out of my mind, but I began to see a red color in Papa, in you, and in Dad. The same color I saw in myself. I knew we were different from the rest of the family, but I also knew I *belonged*. But I didn't understand, so I kept my secrets and never asked. I now need you and Dad to mentor me, teach me the ways, and guide me along the path that I am destined to be on."

Frank hugs his daughter and nods his approval, although he's worried that his daughter is on the same path. Sabrina looks at Kari, then back to her brother, and is pleased. The family has a new special member.

CHAPTER 2

FRANK JAMES IS CONFUSED, happy, and sad, yet determined.

He has been energized by his father's death. Death is demanded by the dark passenger and inner monster, and when death occurs, the monster is satisfied. But it is never satisfied for long.

That Kari is now involved with her own demons makes Frank nervous for her safety, but he is determined to help her as his father helped him. Frank never wanted this for his daughter, but the family gift is not something to deny. It is fate. And it has selected Kari, so Frank will teach Kari the ways of the gift, the ways of the inner monster, the inner demon, the dark passenger. He will teach her all he knows. There are rules, guidelines that George Francis, Frank James, and Sabrina created with the murders they committed. For one thing, no one under eighteen years of age can be harmed: a person must have time to mature. People with a subtle red aura are to be watched, but people with a bright-red coloring are to be eliminated because they have either committed murder or have been mentally cruel, making them unworthy of life. The family's goal is to eliminate those who are unworthy. This inner dark passenger needs to be both controlled and satisfied. Only murder will keep the rage at bay. Yes, Frank will commit fully and help his daughter Kari. But first things first. There is a funeral to arrange.

George Francis's death is attributed to natural causes. Sabrina has mastered the ability to strangle without moving her hands. No strangulation marks were found on George's neck. Frank arranges his father's burial at Cypress Bay Cemetery, interred next to his wife, Gina, who passed away two years ago. The ceremony is attended by George's family, his law firm, and his many friends and clients. George Francis was a popular person in the community, and all attend to pay their respects. At eighty-six, he lived a long and interesting life—more interesting than anyone at his funeral might guess. The family is grateful for George being in their life. His legacy will live on in the family. Along with George Francis, his dark passenger is laid to rest. In the chapel is a color photo of George Francis as a strong man with his trademark white goatee, thin hair, strong firm face, and kind eyes. He looks like the family patriarch that he was.

Frank James thinks, *A fitting end to a person who lived a life full of contradictions. He helped those through his law practice, and he eliminated unworthy people. He rid the earth of bad people; he was not simply a serial killer.*

The family holds hands and prays for his afterlife.

Sabrina holds her secret close, for it was she who brought George's life to an end. She stands at the graveside beside her brother, Frank. She is a handsome woman of thirty, with long black hair, a light complexion, and black eyes. She thinks of her dad, whom she loves, admires, and wants to emulate. His life was complex, as all the lives of the family with the gift must be. Dual lives being lived at the same time. She looks at Kari and is excited about her as an addition.

Kari is fascinated with the burial. A man she loves is interned, but she sees more than a few red swirling colors surrounding the people at the funeral. Her dad and Sabrina for sure, but a few of Papa's friends and clients. Kari is a mature nineteen-year-old with golden red hair, beautiful green eyes, and a resting smiling face. Her lips are never without ruby-red lipstick. She is striking but never calls undue attention to herself. She can blend in whenever she wants.

Looking around at the people at the graveside, Kari smiles as she views his attorney friends and acquaintances, who all seem to have degrees of red in their auras. *Ha! Attorneys*, she thinks. *Who would have guessed?* She must ask her dad about these people. Are they all people who need to die? She is unsure but curious.

The next day, Kari and Sabrina meet with Frank James in his home office. His office is bigger than George Francis's, with more seating, beautiful ocean views from the windows, and vibrant artwork covering the walls.

Frank is sixty-five and in his final years of being a detective with the local police department. He has his dad's trademark white goatee and a head of black hair heavily streaked with gray, which gives him a distinguished look. His blue eyes are framed by black glasses, making him look like a college professor. He has had a colorful career and one of honor. His many awards are displayed on a shelf, taking up a small but important place in both his life and office.

Frank takes a moment to look out the large windows of his home office, taking in the ocean view, the sunny day, and the peace that surrounds him outside. He swivels his office chair back to face the room, where his peace is interrupted by his duty. The family gift requires concentration and discipline. The inner monster, the dark passenger, requires death, and they cannot be denied.

He begins, "Sabrina, Kari, the three of us are now the only members of the family that have the gift."

Kari interrupts, "Dad, this gift, does it not require only the death of one person to fulfill our destiny? It seems Papa and you two have killed beyond that."

Sabrina looks at Frank and answers, "We have a need to see death up close and personal, but once that murder takes place, we then choose to continue to murder and honor our dark passenger. We kill those that meet certain requirements. Those that murder and those that create mental abuse."

Kari says, "And those are identified as being red?"

"Yes," says Frank, "and we are ourselves red, but that color does not come into our lives until we are ready to kill."

"Okay, but how do we overpower others?" asks Kari. "And by what means?"

Frank says, "My father provided us with his special brown liquid that we administer with a shot to the neck. That person has all their senses, but their body will not help them. They are rendered immobile, unable to talk. We are blessed to have this concoction; it is our friend when needing to incapacitate a worthy victim, and then we determine the best method to kill based on our target and the kind of person they are. The kill reverberates throughout the family with the gift, and all feel the power of the kill. It energizes us all."

Sabrina says, "Kari, this family gift is also a burden. We must never, and *I mean never*, divulge this to other family members, especially our children and spouses."

Frank says seriously, "Sabrina and Kari, you are not yet married, but you must make a pledge *here and now* that you will never give up this secret, that you will carry it all your life, never to reveal it to anyone who does not have the gift. We must protect our mission, our destiny, and our family. My wife, Carla, knows nothing of my secret life. Being a detective with the police department is a good cover. Carla must never know."

Frank continues, "Kari, you should think about what course in life will help to protect your secret. Maybe being a lawyer would be good cover."

Sabrina says, "We must be smart and spread out the murders. We cannot have all murders around our community. We must be disciplined about this."

Frank continues, "Sabrina, you must be looking if your father, sister, or brother starts to show red. They may develop the family gift at some point. We are still learning about our gift and what might trigger its appearance."

Sabrina nods, then addresses Kari. "I know this is coming at you fast, but because you are one of us now, you need to know all that we can teach you. We will teach you the ways, the guidelines, and the rules of eliminating someone. Murder is a scary business, and many things can go wrong. We never know how things will go, even with meticulous planning, and the rules for eliminating someone must be suited to each individual. We must always be careful and help each other when that is required."

Frank says, "Kari, death is all around us every day. Our world kills every day. We kill cattle and chickens for food; we kill insects by the thousands each day to protect our vegetables. Military battles throughout the world eliminate people every day. Murderers kill every day. Gangs run wild in our inner cities, killing at random or to be part of a club. Death is all around us. But what we do is right; our killings have meaning.

"Everyone in our sphere is a potential victim. We have set only one rule. The victim must be older than eighteen. Younger children need a chance to grow, to experience life to begin to feel the human spirit. Race and gender have no protection from us.

"Why do we feel this need, this destiny? We don't know, but we've been chosen to do this. There could be other families experiencing this gift."

Frank asks Kari if she understands this complicated subject, and she nods. He continues, "All we know is that once we are selected, we must perform this dance of death. Our dark passenger, our quiet rage, requires it."

Sabrina butts in, saying, "The three of us must answer an array of questions before we murder. How do we kill someone? Do we use a gun, a knife, or rope? How do we get rid of a body? Bury it? Cut it up? How do we deal with blood? And the cleanup? How do you move a body? What if the victim fights back? What if I die trying to murder someone? Will I get seen?"

Frank James looks hard at his niece and his daughter and says, "We cannot go to prison. That is a world of dangerous people, unafraid to kill. And DNA! This is a big deterrent to murder. Leaving a clue, a fingerprint, a piece of hair, or a drop of blood all lead to prison. There is a lot that can go wrong."

Sabrina says, "The first, most important task is to properly identify your target. The faint-red people are going down the wrong path but can still be saved. A strong red signal indicates the most dangerous people who have committed a crime against humanity. These are the people to choose your victim from." Sabrina brushes her hair back and adds, "We must confide in each other. Trust each other. And help each other when the need for help is required. We have been entrusted with a serious task in this life. We must be careful, trust each other, and do what is required of us. We must fulfill our destiny without revealing our calling to another soul outside of those family members with the gift. Our fate has been determined."

Kari feels she now understands and is excited to start her new life now out in the open with her father and her cousin.

CHAPTER 3

FOR HER WHOLE LIFE, Kari has felt different, and now all this information is making her whole. She now realizes that there are others who have the same feelings, the same desires.

She looks at her cousin, Sabrina, who is also listening intently to Frank. Sabrina has committed that one up close and personal murder of her papa, George Francis. She now understands why; it now makes sense. Kind of. Kari needs time to think and absorb all this information. It's information she has wanted all her life, but now she has it; she is both excited and confused.

Frank interrupts Kari's thoughts and says, "I have been following a red person for a couple of weeks now and feel he is my next target. I will continue to follow him and tell you both what I decide, and we can develop a plan to eliminate him. Kari, this is for you to observe. Sabrina, this will give you valuable information on your quest for further targets."

Frank knows it's a lot of information for one day. So much to learn and to know. He is concerned his daughter is now in this lifestyle, and it's his job to train her, guide her, and share all that he knows. He must teach the next generation if this family's gift is to continue. A day will come in the future when Kari will need to survive without him. He must teach her well.

CHAPTER 4

LIFE MUST CONTINUE.

Kari is now in college studying law at a large campus with ivy-covered buildings. As she studies, she knows she must lead two lives and tell no one about her secret life. Everything about her college life is exciting.

Meanwhile, Sabrina has gone back to her passion of writing murder mysteries. Now, she is in her quiet office, in her leather chair, with notes and papers everywhere as she starts a new story. She looks out of her window, watching as people walk past. She certainly will have much more to include in her books now that life has changed forever.

Frank continues to work as a detective, happy to be concentrating on work again. His office building has a cottage-style architecture, wonderful landscaping, and a police interior full of desks and busy people. Frank has a comfortable corner office with large windows that let in plenty of the day's sun. Frank had two murders he was working on before his father's death. He goes back to these cases that his partner, Michael Jacobson, has been working on during his absence. Michael is a tall, broad-shouldered man standing an impressive six feet three with an infectious grin and an easygoing personality. Today, he wears dark slacks, a white shirt with blue stripes, and his customary blue vest. He walks over to Frank, who is dressed in brand-new blue jeans and a starched white shirt.

"Hey, boss," says Michael with a big smile, happy to see Frank back at his desk. "So sorry about your dad. He was a great guy and always treated me well. I know you must miss him."

"Thanks, Michael," Frank says, pleased to see his colleague too. "Where are we with the Max Jefferson homicide?"

Michael says, "DNA on the murder weapon came back. We've picked up the perp, and the DA thinks it's a slam-dunk case. Regarding the Mike Westwood case, the cause of death was poisoning. Ethylene glycol was found in high quantities in his blood. It appears he was served antifreeze in his drinks. His wife, Liz, denies it, but all roads lead to her. She also had a million-dollar life insurance policy on his life that she took out three months ago."

"Great," says Frank. "Looks like we are mostly on top of the current case load. We can start looking at some of the cold cases. You pick a couple, and I'll pick a couple, and let's see if we can make any progress."

Frank starts looking at an old case of the murder of Phyllis Granger, twenty-four, who was molested, murdered, and dumped in the ocean. The postmortem suggested something, probably an anchor, was tied to her body but slipped off. No one was held responsible for her death.

Frank James pores over the case files for days, examining every last detail. The case is four years old, and while reading the files and reports, he comes across an interesting detail. A man was seen with the victim at the marina the week before Phyllis disappeared, but he had left the marina on the boat he was living on and was considered long gone. For whatever reason—laziness or lack of resources—this lead was not followed. The man's name is Jack Evans, age twenty-eight. Frank has a feeling this Jack fellow may have been involved. If this man is responsible, Frank is sure he'll know it when he presses him. A murder this cruel must have been carried out by someone with a powerful red aura.

He thinks of involving Sabrina and Kari but must first check out his hunch. Sabrina says, "It seems like we should go to the marina and see if Jack Evans is there or if anyone there has seen him."

Kari says, "I could stroll around the marina looking for his boat or any signs of him."

Frank says, "Let me do the first review of the marina. Remember, this man is dangerous. I'll let you know what I find."

He hangs up from the girls. "Hey, Michael," Frank says. "I'm going out to the marina to follow a lead on the Granger case. Call me if you need anything."

"Right, boss," Michael replies.

Frank is disturbed that Jack Evans had left the marina and no follow-up had been noted in the file. It's a problem Frank needs to correct immediately. Frank is familiar with the Parkside Marina, as he keeps his Formula 350 Sun Sport boat there. He wishes he could spend more time on the boat, but life is busy. First, Frank visits his cherry-red boat and sees that it looks great and that the marina boat company is keeping his boat "in the ready." Then he sets about trying to find Jack Evans.

He looks up and down the docks for anyone seeming to be living on a boat. After a few minutes, he spots an old, abused twenty-eight-foot Olga trawler, which seems to have someone living there. The slip where the boat is docked shows that the boat has recently been out to sea. Frank notices that there are two unused small anchors tied to the bow of the boat. *Interesting*, thinks Frank. Why would a boat this size have such small anchors? They certainly would not be useful to this vessel.

Frank is studying the boat when a man in his early thirties, the right age for Jack Evans, opens the door with his coffee, walks to a chair, and plops down. Frank observes that the man is about five feet ten in height, with dirty, unkempt blond hair and a concave torso, which makes him look like he needs a large meal. He does not see Frank on the boardwalk adjacent to the boat.

"Morning," says Frank.

The man turns and says, "Good morning to you too."

Jack has a bright white smile, but that cannot detract from his aura. Frank notes the man is red. A deep red.

"Been living on this boat long?" asks Frank.

"Yeah, about six years, but I voyage out now and then up and down the coast."

"Got a boat myself," says Frank.

"I love the freedom of being able to pull anchor and find new places to settle. Always end up back here, though." The man smiles. "Something keeps calling me back."

"So, no job?" asks Frank.

The man looks at Frank warily, seeming to wonder why this stranger is taking an interest, but then he shrugs and replies, "I can make a pretty good living right on my boat. I have a podcast, actually."

"Great! Can I listen?"

"Sure, it's called 'On the Water with Jack Evans.' You're a boat guy; maybe you've heard of it?"

"No, I haven't, but I sure will give it a listen."

"Appreciated," says the man. "I'm Jack, by the way."

"Frank," says Frank. "Detective Frank from the nineteenth precinct."

Jack suddenly looks uneasy.

"What brings you down here?" Jack asks Frank.

"I came to check on my own boat, but I'm looking into a murder that happened about four years ago. Phyllis Granger. Ever heard of her?" says Frank.

Jack shrugs. "Name doesn't ring a bell."

But Frank sees Jack's red aura intensify, burning brighter. He has his answer. Frank has his man, and he knows it. So does his man, Jack Evans. But Frank knows he needs proof.

"All right, I'll see you around, then," says Frank.

Jack sips his coffee as he watches the detective retreat, his mind racing.

Jack *must* escape this detective, but he has a few things to clear up before he can leave. He needs diesel fuel, and he has to pay back rent on the slip before the marina will let him leave. He goes to the office and assures the manager he will leave the rent in the office drop box along with money for the fuel and tells them he will not be there in the morning but will be all paid up. They agree, warning him they will call the authorities if he doesn't deliver on his promises.

But now he needs money, and in Jack's world, the only way to get money is to steal someone else's. Podcasting isn't the moneymaker he'd hoped, not by a long way. He will troll the streets tonight to come up with the six hundred dollars he will need to escape this detective. He did it before, when detectives nosed around, and he will do it again. After a while, when the heat is off, he can come back to Parkside Marina where pretty girls and money are both always available.

Frank watches from a hillside and knows Jack is about to flee. He checks with the marina office and knows Jack is behind in rent and has little fuel to go far, but he can be out of there within a few days. Frank must act immediately, or Jack and his trawler will slip through the net again.

But first, Frank looks up the make and model of the two anchors he saw on the boat. At the local marina store, he finds out that Jack ordered and purchased three anchors a year ago. Frank goes back to the file and finds out the anchor chain on the deceased girl matches the other two anchors. Frank knows he could simply have Jack arrested. He has enough evidence to hold him in custody and have him charged. But Jack is a slippery fish whom Frank cannot afford to lose again, and prison will only make Jack Evans meaner, nastier, and more dangerous. No, it's better to take this man out of action entirely; the world will be a better place.

Jack knows how to make some quick money. A proficient thief and gold digger, he successfully maintains a good lifestyle by stealing from and cheating the young women. Jack puts on a clean jacket, combs his mop of hair, and splashes on some Obsession cologne. "Looking good, my man," he says to himself in the mirror before he leaves his boat for an evening of pirating, on the hunt for a sweet treasure chest.

Jack leaves the marina and heads downtown in the early evening. Bars and dives are his destination; stealing money is his goal. And he is good at it. The money is as good as his.

Frank, Sabrina, and Kari meet at the marina. Frank has given them a detailed briefing of the Granger murder and Jack's role in it. Both Sabrina and Kari are all in on the mission to rid the world of Jack Evans, a dangerous man. As instructed by Frank, Sabrina is wearing a sexy red silk dress, ready to perform her role in the plan, while both Frank and Kari are in work clothes.

Seeming casual to any observer, Frank, Sabrina, and Kari go confidently aboard Jack's boat, as if they've been invited. The outside of the boat is run-down, but the inside of the vessel is modern, with fresh paint. Frank goes down to the engine room below deck. He works hard to open up eight-inch holes in three different places on the bottom of the hull. He quickly and expertly fills the holes with a hot wax mixture he has brought with him that keeps the water out. For now. Frank worries that Jack may come back early, so he is quick with his work.

Meanwhile, Kari and Sabrina go to the bedroom and work diligently to hide two devices on the bed frame. They are uneasy and a bit worried that this will actually work.

Sabrina and Kari wait for Frank on his cherry-red Formula boat, *Red Demon*. When Frank returns, they try to relax, but Sabrina and Kari are nervous. But they are also experiencing emotions of glee and excitement: a kill is underway. The energy is palpable.

Hours later, Jack Evans returns and goes to the marina office to deposit an envelope filled with cash for the back rent and for the diesel fuel. Sabrina is waiting on the dock for Jack to pass by. He is walking back to his trawler when he spots Sabrina in a red silk dress sitting on the back, or stern, of a boat quietly crying.

"Whoa, what's up? Why is a pretty girl like you sitting on a boat crying? What can I do to help?" Jack says with little sympathy and a lot of lust. He doesn't care why she's crying, but crying girls are easy, so he's hopeful his night will end with more than stolen cash. A damsel in distress. Jack is very interested.

"I was supposed to meet someone here an hour ago, but they haven't shown up or called," Sabrina says, trying to sound meek.

"Well, whoever he is must be an idiot," says Jack cheerily. "It's a good thing I'm here because I have a boat just down the dock where you can warm up and we can have a drink to forget our troubles. How does that sound?"

"You know, that sounds great," says Sabrina. "I'm Kaytlin, by the way."

"Jack," he replies. "At your service."

If Sabrina couldn't see his red aura, she might have thought he was being friendly and gentlemanly. Of course, she agrees to follow him along the dock and onto the boat. Her heart thumps hard, but she feels in control with Frank and Kari standing by.

Once on the boat, Jack asks her what she wants to drink.

"Oh, I don't know. Whatever you like," she says, hoping to sound meek again. Best to let Jack think he's in charge.

"I'm going to make you an Old Fashioned," he says. "Because I'm an old-fashioned kind of guy."

Old-fashioned woman hater, Sabrina thinks, watching him make the drinks.

As he puts the drinks together, he tells her, "I was going to go for a moonlight cruise. Would you like to go, Kaytlin?"

"I'd love to, but I need to be back here in a few hours," says Sabrina.

"Then it's settled," Jack says, handing her the drink he's made.

They talk for a while before Jack maneuvers the boat out of the marina and into the beautiful moon-bright ocean. An hour or so passes, and Jack is quite tipsy. Sabrina has managed to remain sober, which helps her fend off Jack's advances firmly but without angering him. She flirts enough to keep him sweet, but after a while the tactic begins to wear off.

"Come on," Jack says. "You've enjoyed my hospitality, so now it's time I got something."

He leads her by the hand to the bedroom, which is where Sabrina needs him to be for the next part of the plan. *It's a good thing men are so predictable*, she thinks. He climbs onto the bed and beckons her to join him. Pretending to be coy, she complies, but she sits with her back to him. "You're too drunk," she tells him.

Rejection angers him, and he lunges for her, grabbing and ripping her flimsy red silk dress. She is expecting it, so she is prepared. Jack is in a rage, but so is Sabrina. Her inner monster is at the ready, and she hits Jack hard to get him off her. Sabrina discovers she has the inner monster at her disposal. Strong, unrelenting, and aggressive. It takes over her limbs and gives her a strength she has never felt before. The protective inner monster had not been needed when she killed Papa, so its arrival at this moment is a joy and a relief. With her newfound power, she hits Jack hard.

Jack is stunned. Never has a girl fought back, and certainly not such a strong, determined girl. *She just signed her death warrant. I'm going to kill her and dump her in this cold ocean just as I've done before,* Jack thinks.

But while Jack is stunned, Sabrina reaches down and grabs the things she and Kari had hidden earlier: two pairs of handcuffs secured to a solid metal rod that holds the bed in place during rough seas. Deftly, she secures his left hand into the handcuffs and closes it tight, then secures his left foot in the other handcuff.

He is captured. And he is angry. "What the hell? Get me out of these! You can't drive this boat. You need me."

"Oh, but I don't," says Sabrina.

Sabrina signals Frank and Kari with a flashlight, who pull up in the *Red Demon*. They climb aboard and hand Sabrina fresh clothes. Frank looks at Jack and says, "Jack Evans, you are about to have a horrible time. You know how you left Phyllis Granger in the ocean to fend for herself and who knows how many more before her? Well, you are about to experience what they experienced."

Frank is pleased with his plan, and it is already working. The boat is much lower in the water than it should be, so he knows the holes in the boat are now letting in water. He points this out to Jack, who begins to struggle more in his handcuffs.

"The water will continue to rise over you, and you will die a slow, awful, uncomfortable, cold death," Frank says.

Frank is invigorated with this kill, ecstatic, bubbling with raw energy. Sabrina is trembling with excitement. Kari, too, is experiencing the thrill of a kill. Their dark passengers are all pleased.

"Goodbye, Jack Evans. You are done," says Frank.

Jack is angry but terrified. He knows he is in big, big trouble. He screams in frustration. "I'll get out of this," Jack says without conviction. He is done for and knows it.

It is time for the family to return to the *Red Demon*. Before Sabrina leaves, she turns to Jack and says in a strong, forbidding voice, "And Jack, my name is Sabrina, not Kaytlin; remember that as you leave this world. *Sabrina*. And remember Phyllis too."

Jack Evans has one hour to live.

He is afraid; it is dark on his boat, and the only sound he can hear is the chugging of the engine slowly taking him further from land. He is handcuffed to his bed. He laughs a tearful laugh; the bed that has brought him so much pleasure, and the bed where many young women have died. He is now secured to this bed with no way out.

The water is beginning to creep into the boat. The boat is listing to the right. He knows his time is short. The cold water slowly envelops his back and shirt. Fear creeps into his mind. A dark, horrible fear.

CHAPTER 5

TIME MARCHES FORWARD. Frank, Sabrina, and Kari are seasoned and knowledgeable in the ways of the family gift, continuing to make rules and guidelines for future family members with the gift. Sabrina is happy with the elimination of Jack Evans, and her inner beast is pleased. Life seems good for the moment. Kari is also happy to have experienced this team effort. She is learning the gift and is in a good place in life. She has just turned twenty-three and is now both a full member of the family "kill team" and almost finished with law school. She is learning her new trade with a law firm. The law school building is old and ivy-covered. The old building is fitting for the oldest profession. At least one of them.

As a criminal law student, Kari is noticed by professors for her intelligence and insights. Professor Tony Romano is a formal-looking professor who always wears a tie and vest with a dark brown beard. One day, he pulls Kari aside at the end of her last law class for the day.

"Kari, I have been noticing you, and you seem to glow when capital murder or a death penalty case is discussed. You have good arguments in the class discussion. Since you're just about to graduate, I want to offer you employment at my law firm, Romano, Murphy, & Erickson. You'd be taking on the defense of clients. It is hard work, long hours, but it is rewarding when you can get someone cleared when they are not guilty."

Kari is surprised but not shocked. She knows she is a good student, but the offer is one to think about. "Thank you, Professor Romano. I hadn't made my mind up about joining the prosecution or defense team in my career, but I've been leaning toward defense. So, yes, I'd like to take you up on your offer for employment."

Tony says, "We are a diverse firm, as our name reflects. Italian, Irish, and Swedish. It makes us all laugh, but at the same time we are serious, and you will be exposed to a lot of wildly different cases. Pass your final exam, then come see me."

And that is what she does. The Romano, Murphy, & Erickson law firm is situated in the center of downtown, in a distinctive round three-story building with forty-five other attorneys. She works directly with Tony Romano, who teaches her the art of defending people, even when they appear to be guilty. She is learning the tricks of the trade and is quickly becoming an important player in the office, not yet taking on clients on her own but gaining ground as "second chair" on cases.

Her latest case involves a banker, Jerry O'Brien, who is laundering money through his firm, Taylor Creek Central Bank. He takes in money from a local woman, a drug dealer, Payton Riley, and disguises the financial assets so they can be used without detection of illegal activity. He is guilty, but Kari and her team win Frank O'Brien's case, and he is not convicted. A big win, indeed. Payton Riley is not convicted either and is still doing illegal activity without the use of Taylor Creek Central Bank. She's a small-time crook but with big-time ambitions. She has a big hold on the drug business in the area, and she is mean and dangerous. She will not hesitate to eliminate competition or threats to herself. People in the locality are dying daily doing drugs supplied by Payton Riley. When Kari sees Payton Riley's bright red aura, Kari's demon wakes, thirsty for a kill. Kari thinks that she must have the dark passenger in her because her response to Payton is calculating, determined, and patient.

Kari tells Sabrina about her thoughts, and Sabrina agrees Payton needs to be eliminated. They discuss how to get her in a situation where she is alone and get rid of her. But how? Payton is a dangerous person, and the people she associates with in the drugs trade are dangerous too. They need to think long and hard on how to eliminate her. Pushing her off a rocky cliff into the ocean? Sabrina shakes her head, fearful about being pulled over the edge by Payton or Payton surviving the fall into the ocean. No, a better plan is needed. A fail-safe plan.

Kari gets information about Payton Riley from the office files. Knows where she lives and knows where she works out of. She also has her personal phone number. Sabrina and Kari watch Payton for a week. She is five feet tall, loves to dress in all black with long earrings, and has dirty blond hair. Attractive but more dangerous and not someone to walk up to casually to have a conversation. It is obvious that Payton is at the top of a small gang and that she trusts no one with the merchandise. She buys the drugs herself and then distributes them to her gang of sellers who target college campuses, selling to young adults excited to be "finding themselves" using illegal substances. Problem is, the kids want more and more, and some of them overdose and die. Payton does not care. She only wants the money, fame, and power.

Sabrina learns Payton's daily habits. Her source of drugs is a Mexican cartel, La Aguila, "the Eagle." She works only with a man named Carlos Lopez, and the drugs are always transported from different locations: a shed, a field, the beach, and remote locations. Carlos Lopez leaves the merchandise, and it's later picked up by Payton. This gives Sabrina and Kari an idea: They will create a pickup point where Payton will get more than she bargained for.

On a dark, moonless night, Sabrina and Kari dig a small tunnel in the firm sand beside the seawall on Twelfth Street Beach. The digging is slow going, and both Kari and Sabrina are fearful the tunnel will collapse as they dig. It is hard, sweaty work despite the nighttime breeze that blows in off the ocean. Sabrina holds on to Kari's feet as she digs deeper into the tunnel. They are both worried it could collapse at any time. When they finish the construction, both are tired but excited about what is about to happen. The dark passenger waits in anticipation of a kill.

Kari leaves a bogus message on Payton's phone using a burner phone of her own, pretending to be an operative of Lopez.

Kari turns to Sabrina and says, "I'm nervous this won't work."

Sabrina replies, "The waiting is always a restless time for me. You never really get used to it."

The two hide in the darkness under a Monterey cypress tree, waiting for Payton to arrive for an hour. Finally, a shadow comes along the dark beach. They watch Payton casually walk the beach until she comes to a sand tunnel. She looks right and left. There is no one around. She looks around one more time, then gets on her belly and crawls into the sand entry. Watching from a distance, Kari imagines her muttering, "Carlos Lopez is crazy for having me in here and crazy for digging this stash spot."

Meanwhile, Payton is crawling into the tunnel, agitated and tense, thinking, *I hate this. This is scaring me to death. I'm getting in and out as quick as I can.*

When she is about seven feet in the claustrophobic sand tunnel, Kari and Sabrina come out of hiding and jump hard on the top of the sand cave. It does not budge. They panic. They jump with all their might and weight. Sabrina says, "Jump harder, Kari; put all your weight in it." Sabrina is jumping up and down as hard as she can. Payton tries to scream and move. Suddenly, the sand cave collapses. Payton is trapped without light and without air, soon also without hope.

Payton Riley has four minutes to live.

Her mouth and nose are full of sand; she cannot breathe and chokes when she tries to. She is paralyzed by the heavy sand. She is dying and knows it.

Above ground, Kari looks at Sabrina and says breathlessly, "Oh my God, we did it. I can't believe it worked."

Sabrina replies, "It is a thrilling feeling when your planning works, when your plan comes together and a bad person is eliminated. What we do is worthy. You did good, girl. You did not hesitate."

They wait until they can no longer feel any struggle under the sand. The tide will be in soon, battering the seawall, and Payton's body will be released from its sand coffin to be found. Her small but deadly drug empire is no more.

The monsters that reside in Kari and Sabrina are satisfied. The thirst is quenched. The dark passengers are happy. For now. Sabrina and Kari walk away quickly from the death scene, get into their waiting car, and drive away. Mission accomplished. They are thrilled but exhausted. Eliminating someone always is a hard experience. A life is no more. A good kill, but a kill nevertheless, is something to be respected.

Early the next day, Frank, Sabrina, and Kari are in Frank's office talking about the demise of the drug dealer. Kari concludes, "I couldn't believe it worked. She went right into her death chamber looking for drugs. Drugs that were never there. The feeling I had throughout my body was electric."

Frank asks, "Did you be sure not to leave any evidence, anything the police can use to catch you?"

"No, we were cautious and left nothing for the police to find. We are safe," says Sabrina.

Kari adds, "We were very careful not to leave any clues as to what happened there. The police will be baffled when they do find her."

Both Sabrina and Kari are abuzz telling the tale to Frank. The demons are pleased.

Kari says, "I can only imagine how Payton felt. She was all alone in that dark death trap. But I was alive with emotions."

"Me too," Sabrina says.

Frank says, "I can hear in your voices and see looking at both of you that this was a *good* kill. A red person gone forever. Young people around here are safer. You two go now and get back to your lives. Remember not to discuss this with anyone, ever."

After both women have left Frank's office, he sits in his leather chair staring out at the rolling ocean waves, his thumb under his chin and his forefinger on his lip. Life without his father is strange, but the family is moving on, and the hunt for red people deserving justice is foremost on their minds. *I think George Francis would be proud of the family*, he muses.

A week later, when Kari is at work, her boss, Tony Romano, calls her into his office. With him are two police detectives from the drug enforcement task force along with Anna Romano, Tony's wife and office manager.

Tony starts, "Kari, please sit down. These detectives and Anna have some questions for you."

"Certainly, whatever I can do to help. Can you tell me what this is all about?" asks Kari.

The first detective says, "I am Dean Wilson, and this is my partner, Ben Holloway. We have been following a local drug dealer named Payton Riley who's distributing drugs to the young adults in the area. We know she works with Carlos Lopez through a Mexican cartel, La Aguila. Both have been under surveillance, but Payton has disappeared within the last week. We can't seem to locate her. Anna told us you worked on a case involving Payton Riley and that you were vocal about her getting away without prosecution. We want to know what you might know about this."

The other detective adds, "Anna says you told everyone on the case that 'she would get hers' in the near future. Kari, did you have anything to do with Payton Riley's disappearance? Or do you know anyone else who might be involved in her disappearance?"

Kari is startled and knows her cheeks are flushed, but Frank warned her that a follow-up by police may be a possibility, so she calms her breathing as the detectives are talking, and the heat in her face begins to cool.

With an air of confidence, she says, "I have no idea what happened to Payton. I did feel regret that she got away with her money laundering scheme, and I did blow off some steam about her getting her just deserts, but I would never do anything about it myself. I work within the rules, detectives." Of course, by the "rules," she is talking about the family kill rules. She is telling the truth, and she hopes the cops will take the "truth" at face value and back off.

Ben Holloway asks, "You had access to the Payton file?"

"Almost everyone in this office has access," Kari replies, glancing at Anna with a frown.

"Okay, ma'am. I hope we don't see another connection with you as we look further into her disappearance," says Detective Holloway. "Good day."

He says goodbye to Anna, adding, "Thank you; we'll be in touch."

When the detectives have left, Anna turns to Kari and says, "I only pointed out that you were concerned about the verdict and may have looked into the files."

"I understand," says Kari and leaves the office, her heart still pumping hard.

Kari now knows why the family is so concerned with leaving clues for the police. They are professionals with a lot of experience in crime scenes. Even the smallest clue will have the police looking deeply into it. She heads to the restroom and stands in a stall, shaking slightly. *Gotta be careful, girl*, she thinks.

That night after work, Kari calls Frank and meets him at his home office. Kari, sitting with her father and Sabrina, is uneasy. She tells them about the events of the day.

Frank says, "None of us can be caught or even be suspected. It will bring all of us down. I'll talk to detectives Wilson and Holloway and let them know you are my niece and to look elsewhere for any information on the disappearance of Payton Riley."

Kari is relieved that Frank will help divert attention away from her, but she is determined never to put herself in that position again.

CHAPTER 6

THE YEARS ARE PASSING. Frank, now seventy-three, is retired, but he keeps close to the police department. Detective Michael Jacobson calls Frank often to talk and asks his opinion about ongoing cases. This keeps Frank current on police matters.

Both Kari and Sabrina are married now. Sabrina met Sam Jefferson, a firefighter and paramedic, at Kari's wedding to Jason Dempsey. Sam's opening line was, "Well, hello, beautiful," and Sabrina had replied, "Well, hello yourself." The relationship was a whirlwind, and they married only eight months later. Before they married, Sam asked Sabrina if she had any deep, dark secrets he should know about. She'd winked at him and told him, "I sure do, but they will stay deep and dark." She laughed, but she was deadly serious; she could never tell Sam about that side of her life. Never. Sam isn't even the lightest shade of red. Sabrina and Sam quickly had two children, Lyndsey and Tiffany Rose. When they were born, Sabrina saw that both were a slight shade of red, and Sabrina often wonders if either will follow in her footsteps. Lyndsey and Tiffany Rose are growing up in a wonderful world of family and friends and in safety. The world is not safe, but the family is doing what they can to make it a better place by taking out the people in the community who are dangerous.

Kari married Jason Dempsey, a pilot for companies and wealthy individuals and celebrities. They are thrilled to have one son, Nelson. Like Sabrina, Kari also keeps a keen eye on her family. She thought she saw a wispy red on Jason when they first met. It was what attracted her to him, but she could not figure out why. Ordinarily, red people are to be *dealt with*, but something about Jason is familiar and comforting. He's a fun, loving husband, but he does not know of Kari's family gift. Kari will never tell him. This is a family secret, not to be discussed outside of the family with the gift. Kari sees the smallest wisp of red on her son Nelson from time to time but thinks little of it while he's so young.

One day, Kari and Sabrina are investigating a woman with a bright red glow. Her name is Roberta Jones, a physical therapist treating wealthy people. While she treats her clients, she gathers key information about them, such as the state of their finances and what other assets they own, including their homes. When a wealthy client ends their physical therapy session, Roberta has enough information to go after them.

Roberta Jones is professional during the day but a terror at night. She disguises herself and invades the homes of her clients, stealing from them, often violently, physically abusing them without any thought to what she is doing to their lives. She is making quite a sum of money from older ex-clients who are less able to fight back. She is not afraid to hurt these older citizens, and she is able to scare them into not going to the police.

From their surveillance, Sabrina and Kari find Roberta has a pattern. She disguises her looks, puts on a pretty dress, and then goes to former clients' homes. When they answer the door to her, she acts like an old acquaintance, which confuses them. This woman looks familiar to them, so surely they know her? But out of the context of the therapists' office, and in everyday clothes rather than her PT uniform, the elderly folk cannot easily place her. On the few occasions when the person at the door recognizes her, she claims she has dropped by to see how her former patient is getting on. Then she can walk away. But where there is confusion, she pounces. She talks her way into their homes, and the moment the door closes behind her, she turns on her victim. During the time she's there, she intimidates her victims and makes them open their safes. She steals their money, jewelry, and valuable possessions. She ties up her victims, then returns home, where the first thing she does is take a long, hot shower.

Sabrina and Kari decide it's time Ms. Jones meets her maker, and Kari has been planning the sting operation. She's nervous and afraid but knows what her inner beast, her dark passenger, requires her to do, and what her family is committed to: ridding the earth of unworthy people.

On the chosen evening, Kari goes to Roberta's house and waits for her to go out. They know that this is the day of the week when Roberta likes to carry out her crimes, and they are not disappointed. She emerges from the house in her subtle disguise and heads out. Kari and Sabrina feel bad that someone might get hurt tonight at Roberta's hands, but they hope that whoever it is will be the last one to suffer.

The moment Roberta drives away, Kari makes her move. Going around the back of the house, she puts on plastic shoe covers on her feet, then puts on thin rubber gloves. Then she carefully works the door lock, like her father has taught her. She is on edge but finally gets the lock to release. She opens the door and rushes in and, with her back to the door, catches her breath. Then she sets about her plan. She heads straight for the bathroom and takes out of her pocket a small bottle of clear oil and smears it all over the tiled bathroom floor, still wearing the disposable gloves. She looks around to be sure she has not left any indication she was there. Then she hides in the bedroom closet and waits for Roberta's return. Kari hopes that won't be too long.

Roberta returns an hour or so later. She is laughing as she spills the cash and jewelry on the bed and looks admiringly at her night's work before she takes her clothes off and puts them into the washer. Then she walks naked to the bathroom, anticipating her routine shower. But as she steps into the bathroom, she is shocked that the tile is so slippery. She cannot keep her footing and falls hard, flat on her back on the slippery floor. Roberta is stunned for a moment and tries to catch her breath.

Before Roberta knows what's happening, Kari is on top of Roberta, administering a shot to the right side of her neck with the family's secret brown liquid. High on adrenaline, Kari is strong, and she has easily overpowered Roberta, who is shocked that someone is in her home and panicked that she now can't move—not her arms, her legs, nothing.

Kari kneels down with Roberta. Roberta is unable to move, unable to talk, but her mind is wide awake, her eyes taking in everything that is happening. Kari begins, "Roberta, I know all about you. I know who you are and what you've been doing tonight. You are a healer during the day and a devious, dishonest schemer at night, hurting and robbing those that you pretend to help. I am here to eliminate you. You are about to die."

Fear is shining in Roberta's questioning eyes. *What is this? Why are you here? I'm going to die? Here? Now?*

"If there is an afterlife," continues Kari, "you are about to see it. I expect yours will be a bed of nails, not roses."

With that, Kari gives Roberta a second shot. Her breathing accelerates and then begins to slow. The life in her blue eyes begins to fade.

Kari is invigorated. She whispers in Roberta's ear, "I can feel death's power, and I know you can too. Embrace it. You will soon be in the next world."

Roberta has two minutes to live.

Kari looks into Roberta's petrified eyes and tells her, "Goodbye. You have done this to yourself."

Putting her hands around Roberta's neck with a strong grip, she quickens Roberta's demise. Kari and Roberta are in the death dance, and Kari feels more alive as Roberta's death nears. Finally, Kari senses Roberta's soul has been extinguished. She stands over the body, her emotions a tornado inside her. Her demon is excited, her monster happy.

But she cannot stay. The longer she is there, the greater the chance of being caught. Kari rushes from the house, leaving the back door wide open. She removes her shoe coverings and gloves before getting into her car. She'll incinerate these when she gets home.

Roberta is found days later when her neighbors notice a foul smell coming from her home and call authorities, who investigate the murder, discovering in the process that the dead woman was responsible for a string of home invasions. The stolen money, jewelry, and possessions are found and returned to her victims. The cops can't believe their luck to have solved several crimes, but now they are left with a mystery: Who tampered with the door lock, and how did Roberta Jones die? The crime scene investigators find some spilled essential oil on the bathroom floor, which appears to be why she fell, but why did she stop breathing? There are puncture wounds on her neck, but the toxicology report turns up nothing untoward. There are no strangulation marks because Kari has learned the family secret to strangulation. So, Roberta's death is ruled an accident: an accidental fall and heart failure.

CHAPTER 7

FRANK JAMES RETIRED FROM WORK as a police detective, but he has not retired from the family business. His inner monster is hungry, and he knows he must feed it soon. The secret rage is waking up in its secret place and demanding attention.

Frank learns from his friend and former coworker, Michael Jacobson, that there's a serial rapist who has gone underground to evade capture. Frank listens intently to Michael's description of the man, Bernard Baker. His assaults are known to be brutal, and he is a wanted man. He is interested, and his monsters come alive, thirsty for a murder. He can't tell the family about his hunt. They have been telling him to refrain from killing, as he is getting too old, and the chance of leaving a clue or making a mistake is something the family can't have. But he gets on his computer and begins to track Bernard Baker, who goes by his initials to his friends. BB lives here and there, often staying with women he picks up and then discards.

Frank wants to find him first and deal with him directly rather than let him go through a lengthy criminal trial that often takes years. Frank's justice will be swift and permanent. But first he must find him before the police do.

Michael has told him that BB has a medical condition—anemia—that requires him to go to the hospital for treatment. He often has to stay overnight. Frank thinks of both his sister, Betty, and her daughter, Sasha Louise, who work at Kensington Hospital. The only hospital nearby. So, Frank calls Betty. "What can you tell me about patients with chronic anemia?"

Betty replies, "Anemia stops blood from carrying as much oxygen to cells, so people with serious anemia might need blood transfusions to get hemoglobin-rich red blood cells. Some patients get transfusions on a regular basis. Why, what's up?"

"Betty, I'm just looking for someone. I need to talk to him. Does anyone come into the hospital that fits that description?" asks Frank.

"You know I shouldn't give you confidential information, Frank," she says.

"I'm just helping some old colleagues out. Can you just tell me if anyone is being treated with you for that condition? I'll do the rest."

"Actually, yes. I won't give you a name, but there is someone here now."

Frank perks up; his dark passenger is interested.

"Great," says Frank.

"Any chance you know when he'll leave the hospital?"

Betty chuckles. "I'm not telling you anything else. The police will need to deal with this, not cut corners with you, brother."

Frank laughs. His sister hasn't a wisp of red about her; she's a saint. "I appreciate that, Betty. So, tell me, how's the family?"

"The family is fine. Sabrina is writing another murder mystery. Sasha Louise is a registered nurse working with me here, and little George is a physical therapist working close by. I'm semiretired now. Just going home when you caught me," says Betty.

"Thanks, Betty, go home and have your husband fix you a rum and Coke and relax. Talk to you again soon."

Frank hangs up. He goes to his basement, gets a syringe, fills it with the secret brown liquid, and heads out. Twenty minutes later, he is sitting in his car in the Kensington Hospital parking lot waiting for signs of BB. It is a long wait.

Finally, just when Frank is about to give up, BB appears. He glances right and then left and walks quickly to his car. Frank leaps into action and intercepts him. "Excuse me, sir, can you help me find the emergency entrance to this hospital? I'm lost."

BB tries to move away from this stranger, but the moment he turns his back to open his car door, Frank plunges his syringe into Bernard's neck. Bernard slumps forward, leaning against the driver's door. Making sure he's not being watched, Frank drapes one of BB's arms around his shoulder and walks a woozy BB to his own car, managing to get him into the passenger seat before the injection completely paralyzes him, and off they go. Frank is pleased with himself; BB is increasingly immobile but aware.

Frank drives down to the oceanfront and finds a quiet spot to park. The tide is out, the sun is going down, the sunset is beautiful without being spectacular, and the air is cool and getting colder.

Frank tells him, "Bernard Baker, serial rapist. There's no use in denying it; I know who and what you are. My little shot in your neck is preventing you from speech or movement. You can hear me, and I'm sure you want to talk, but no luck, my friend. This is the end of the line for you. Many women will be spared from you because of what I am going to do to you tonight. Here and now. The damage you have done to these young women requires that I treat you with the same brutality and disregard you showed them. You are going to die a long, cold, and awful death. I want you to think, as you are dying, about all the damage you have caused. It is a ripple effect. You've hurt not only the women you've attacked but also their family and friends. These women had no hope, no savior, when they needed help. You, too, will have no hope, no savior when you need help."

With darkness enveloping them, Frank ensures nobody is around before he pulls Bernard from the car and drags him down to a dock. BB is a much slighter man than Frank, making this possible. Had BB been a bigger man, Frank would have needed another plan. Nevertheless, BB gets heavier and heavier on the short journey to the jetty. The tide is out, so getting below the jetty is easy, at least.

Breathing hard with the effort, Frank ties BB to one of the jetty's support columns underneath. BB is tied in a standing position, looking as if he is caught on something rather than tied up. When he is found, it may appear that he simply got caught on something below the deck. Perhaps he was hiding and just got caught up. Frank hopes that is the case. Bernard is thinking, *Please help me, save me. I'll never do anything bad again, I promise.* But his lips are sealed; his thoughts are trapped in his head. He is doomed, and he knows it. His thoughts go dark: *Those women deserved what they got. All of them.*

The tide is beginning to creep up.

Time to go for Frank.

"Bernard, the tide is coming in, so I have to leave, but you are going to stay and slowly drown where you are. You deserve this."

BB's eyes are bursting; his breath is accelerated. He is scared. He knows he is about to die. Bernard knows he is about to drown.

Bernard Baker has two hours left to live.

Frank is delighted that he still has the strength and desire to bring this man to a place where he will die a slow death. Frank knows his own time on this earth is coming to a close. To be able to do this one more time is invigorating and pleasing.

"Bernard Baker, you have maybe two more hours to live. The sedative I gave you will stop you from calling for help or freeing yourself. A long, cold, painful two hours await you. Plenty of time to consider your life and the way you've lived it. Goodbye."

Bernard is shaking both from the cold water creeping up his body and the thought he will be dead soon. His body is useless, but he feels the ice-cold ocean. His mind is working hard to find a way out. But there is none. The ocean waves are getting stronger as he is getting weaker. Death is searching for him.

CHAPTER 8

KARI IS STILL BUZZING WITH EMOTION days after her murder of Roberta Jones: her up-close and personal kill. She thinks, *Alive one minute, then dead for all eternity by my hands. My mind, my body, my being craves this moment. Death is so final, so permanent. Such a magnificent feeling.*

Already her mind is turning to her next mission. Kari is working on another case at her law firm regarding a financial advisor, Ava Kaiser, who has been charged with insider trading. Ava would meet with politicians and other persons of influence to pass on illicit investment tips, including what to invest in and when to sell to make quick but illegal profits. At first, nobody thought to ask how city and county politicians could afford multimillion-dollar properties and second homes at beach, island, or mountain resorts. Finally, someone uncovered the truth. Kari Dempsey is asked to mount Ava's defense.

Kari is not a fan of Ava Kaiser and is sure she is guilty. It irritates Kari that Ava is leaning on her political friends to ensure she is untouchable. Of course, with such powerful allies, she is acquitted, as Kari knew she would be because her political connections protect her. They want her free because she provides them with information not available to the average person. Information that makes them rich.

Kari is glad for the win in court for her professional reputation, and her office is happy with her defense strategy, but Kari feels that Ava Kaiser should have been found guilty and served time for putting regular, everyday investors in difficult financial positions while enriching the political class. Many of her political friends have the distinctive red aura, but Ava is a bright red.

After the not-guilty verdict, life goes back to normal. But Kari is determined that Ava will be the family's next victim. So, one day Kari meets with her father and Sabrina over lunch at Rob & Christine's Charter House beachside restaurant–the family's favorite place to do business other than Frank's office. It is intimate and private, with wonderful ocean views, chandeliers hanging from many different heights, and great food made with love. There she tells them about Ava, noting, "I have to be careful because of the Payton Riley case, where there was a connection to me. I'm sure that the police and my office manager still keep an eye on me. What I'm saying is that I can supply the personal information about Ava, but I need to stay away from the kill."

The word "kill" awakens all their monsters. Their demons are interested. All three feel the familiar, delicious buzzing within. The excitement is growing. Death is just around the corner.

Kari tells Frank all she knows from having had access to all Ava's information. She's sure that plenty of information has been hidden from her and the firm, but she feels certain that Ava is continuing her illegal activities. Frank nods and asks Sabrina to follow Ava for the next week to find out how she is doing business. "We'll meet back at Rob & Christine's in a week to compare notes," he says.

And so, a week later, they are all back again, sitting at the same table looking at the beautiful, calm ocean, and Sabrina is telling them about her findings. "Ava is meeting individually with her *clients* on the train that goes from Revere to Casanova Station. I was able to overhear one of her conversations, and yes, she's definitely still giving insider trading information. They are getting richer by the day." Sabrina's eyes twinkle as she continues, "When I got off the train, I followed the guy she'd been talking to and found out who he is. Since then, I've been sending him anonymous messages telling him that unless he passes on more names of Ava's clients, I'll go to the police and ruin his career."

Frank smiles and claps. "Brilliant work, Sabrina."

Sabrina says, "Thanks. I thought so! He's told me that Ava goes by a code name, 'Silver Spoon,' when she sends messages to her clients so they know it's really from Ava. Without the Silver Spoon name, there is no buy or sell."

The three talk for an hour about their complicated plan, which is due to commence at precisely 10:19 a.m. on Wednesday.

On that day, Frank James, walking unsteadily, dressed as an old man with hearing aids, a heavy coat, and a scarf, gets on the train at Revere Station and sits close enough to hear Ava Kaiser talking to Senator Chester Booth. They pay him no attention as he sits across the aisle. An old man is not a threat to them.

Thanks to her source, Sabrina knows that Ava only puts out her insider tips to no more than ten clients at a time. Just enough to make money but not enough to be worth an investigation. But Sabrina decides to put out a mass message from burner phones to all the contacts she has been given. Every politician who profits from Ava has been contacted. The message reads:

> BREAKING NEWS: Put big money on Swamp Road Industries immediately. 1000% return. Buy by 10:30 am. Sell by 10:55 am. **I have only contacted you.** Don't miss this one. Silver Spoon.

While Ava is whispering to Senator Booth, assuring him that she will continue business as usual but now only on the train, Booth's phone pings. After he reads a message, he turns to Ava and gives her a hard stare.

"Is something wrong, Chester?" she asks.

"This message is from you."

She laughs. "It can't be. I'm right here, and I haven't touched my phone."

"So why the hell have I got a text from Silver Spoon to buy and sell now? What's going on?"

Ava is stunned. "What are you talking about?"

Senator Chester Booth shows his phone with the message from her.

Ava's face is redder than her aura. "No, no, that's not from me. *Don't buy anything.* I know for a fact that Swamp Road Industries is collapsing, and its stock is sinking; it will be worthless very soon."

Ava has four minutes to live.

All of a sudden Ava's phone is ringing, and all her political clients are calling to acknowledge the receipt of their instructions. It's approaching 10:30, when everyone will begin to buy. She cannot message everyone individually in time. They will all lose lots of money, and they will hold her responsible. They won't be able to get their money back, so they will exact payment in other ways and make her life a living hell. Her whole world is unraveling. What can she do?

Ava jumps up from her seat and runs through the railcar. Frank follows her into the vestibule between carriages, where he finds her at the door to the train, trying to open it. She turns and looks at him, frantic. He smiles and says, "There's no other way, Ava Kaiser."

She stares at him as if he's the angel of death. How else can this stranger know her name? She turns back to the door and lowers the window right below that DANGER sign. She cannot get out of the window easily, so she leans out as far as she can while Frank watches, enthralled. All of a sudden, another train passes, taking her head with it. Her decapitated body slumps to the floor. She is gone.

Frank stops. He is stunned.

His inner beast is confused, but all of a sudden, the inner beast is alive. *A suicide.* The demon is thrilled. Frank is vibrating; he is so energized. He calls Kari and Sabrina and tells his story. All the demons are pleased.

Ava Kaiser is dead.

The bent politicians are broke.

The monsters are pleased.

CHAPTER 9

KARI'S PROFESSIONAL LIFE AS AN ATTORNEY IS GOING WELL.

She has become the go-to girl at Romano, Murphy, & Erickson when you need help to get a defendant off. Her successes are noted within the upper echelons of the law firm, which recognizes her talent for the law. They have no idea what else she is talented at.

Her home life is just as satisfying. Her husband Jason is a devoted husband and father. Their son Nelson is growing up and into this and into that. He laughs often and has his father's dark hair. When Jason has on his leather flight jacket and aviator sunglasses, Kari gets flushed and acts like a girl in love. He thinks of himself as a cowboy pilot and will sometimes wear a cowboy hat when he flies.

As a personal pilot, he is gone often but is always in contact with his family. Kari has noticed that when he comes back from a trip flying a variety of celebrities and corporate bigwigs, Jason has a tinge of red about him. It doesn't bother her; rather, she is fascinated and captivated by the wispy red she sees. Her inner beast, her dark passenger, is taking an interest in this information. She asks him questions about his trips from time to time, but he is quite discreet about his private clients and doesn't give much away.

Nelson, too, occasionally shows a soft, very faint redness. This concerns her more than with Jason, and she makes a note to talk to her father and Sabrina about her observations at some point.

One day, Frank, Sabrina, and Kari are meeting in Frank's home office to discuss any current or future targets.

Kari starts, "I have no one specific at this time. There are lots of red candidates in a defense law office, but I have to stay careful."

Sabrina says, "I'm still a struggling writer, but two of my books have been released. *Murder on Rose Lane* and *She Never Saw It Coming: The Rosemary Roberts Story*. Both books are doing okay. Nothing spectacular, but I am making an income. My new book I am writing is based on a true story. It's about an unscrupulous diamond dealer, Sergio Martinez. He sells to wealthy clients, then stages robberies to recover the merchandise, which he then resells. It's based on a seriously red guy I've been following. He's my inspiration for this novel but, more importantly, could be a good candidate for our purposes."

"Interesting," says Frank. "Definitely a person of interest. I, too, have a person that requires elimination. Her name is Emily Carson, and she's the CEO of a large nonprofit, Children's Life, dedicated to helping sick children, especially with brain tumors, HIV, and leukemia."

"She sounds like a good person!" Kari exclaims, worried that her father might be losing his touch and becoming a liability as he ages.

Frank smiles. "Yes, she appears to be. But, in fact, it was your Jason who told me about her. He's flown her to places before and found her wealth suspicious, knowing what she does for a living.

"He suggested she seems to be living a lifestyle that is not reflected in her publicly stated salary. I think she is embezzling funds. The worst thing is she is stealing from the children, denying some children treatment. We need to team up on this case. It's interesting how many large nonprofits have sociopathic CEOs; it's not just the corporate world where this is a problem. They can often get away with it more easily too because nobody wants to threaten the mostly good work of the organization.

“Kari, can you do some research on Emily Carson and her nonprofit organization, Children’s Life?”

Kari agrees.

Then Frank asks Sabrina, “Can you do some surveillance on Emily Carson and see what she’s all about? Where she goes and with whom, what she spends her money on, and who is in her inner circle of friends?”

“Absolutely,” says Sabrina. “This can also be research for a future book!”

“And I’ll look into any criminal activity she may have had in the past or any association with past troubles she may have been involved in,” says Frank. “Let’s meet here in a week to discuss what we find.”

CHAPTER 10

A WEEK LATER, IN FRANK'S HOME OFFICE, Kari reports that Emily Carson has an annual salary of $854,700. She lives in a $3.2 million estate, and she takes extravagant vacations four times a year to the South of France, Italy, Sicily, and Switzerland, and she either travels first class or flies privately. The company she works for, Children's Life, is a $22 million company able to treat 780 children a year. Children's Life collects donations, sometimes large sums of cash, and the accounting is overseen by Emily Carson. Kari concludes, "That by itself is suspicious."

Next, Sabrina tells Frank and Kari what she has discovered during her surveillance, which is that Emily is not married, but she dates regularly, although there's nobody special. She eats out every night at expensive places, orders costly wine, and treats her men and friends well. She dresses in top-of-the-line designer clothes, her home is exquisite inside, and she drives a Tesla X and a Tesla S.

They all agree that this lifestyle isn't possible on her salary, as large as it is.

Frank says, "Emily has a criminal past but nothing that would stop her from being CEO of a company. A few shoplifting charges when she was young and a few bad check charges when she was a little older. Clearly now she's gone big-time."

Sabrina adds, "And now we know from Jason that Emily will be flying with him to Interlaken in Switzerland for a two-week vacation."

Frank says, "Great work, Sabrina. Let me consider the best way forward in light of this information." Sabrina and Kari take a walk along the beachfront for an hour, stopping at a café, to give Frank some time to formulate a plan. When they return, Frank is grinning.

"Sabrina, I want you to go to Interlaken. Friday of this week."

She is surprised. "I'll need to shuffle a few things, but okay."

"I will send Emily Carson an invitation to a paragliding center and make her a discount she can't refuse. I will send her your name, which will be Kelly Taylor, who is an expert paraglider pilot."

As he explains his idea for a paragliding "accident," Sabrina nods her head in agreement, and all the demons awake. A kill is in the air. Even a kill so far away is thrilling and not to be missed. Excitement is building.

High Speed Jet Service, Jason's flight company, meets Emily on the apron at the Jet Center, and a member of the flight crew escorts her and her guest onto the jet. The flight over to Switzerland is uneventful, except that Emily Carson is a demanding customer and requires the flight attendant to bring various meals and champagne and put on this movie, then that show. A clean glass is required, an expensive wine, hors d'oeuvres, etc. The boyfriend, Regan Staples, is amused and laughs at this crazy lady making the flight chaotic. Regan is pleased: an all-expenses-paid trip to Switzerland with a woman who has expensive taste is fine with him, even if she is demanding.

Jason lands the jet expertly at Bern Airport, and Emily and Regan are picked up by a waiting limousine and whisked off to the Linder

Hotel. Sabrina is waiting in the lobby when Emily and Regan enter the hotel, but she keeps her distance. *No need to meet her too soon. I think I'll just watch her for a day or so*, Sabrina thinks.

The weather is beautiful, the snow-covered Alps are spectacular, and the food is wonderful. After three days in this heaven, both Emily and Regan are ready to have some experiences other than the ones they have been having in the hotel room, night and day. Time to get some fresh air and do something else that is stimulating.

Emily reaches into her purse and pulls out the email from Frank posing as someone from a vacation adventure company with a special offer of paragliding while she's in Interlaken. The email had said that this offer was exclusive to High Speed Jet Service customers, so she had taken it at face value, thinking that paragliding would be the kind of thrill she'd enjoy. She looks for a phone number on the printout and then calls Kelly Taylor.

Sabrina answers, "Hello, this is Kelly."

Emily says, "I have been given your information, and I would like to sign up for a ride tomorrow for me and my boyfriend."

Sabrina says, "Tomorrow? Hmmm. Let me quickly bring up my schedule." There's a pause as she pretends to check her availability. "Actually, I had a late cancellation and have an 8:30 slot tomorrow morning. I can offer your boyfriend the same trip at 10:30, after you and I return. The flights last about forty-five minutes from when we lift off. The fee is $450 each. I will need $900 when I pick you up at 8:30."

"I have a fifty percent discount offer through High Speed Jet Service," says Emily.

"That will be for one person. So that would be $675 for you both. I prefer cash," Sabrina says.

"Cash?" Emily asks. "That's rather inconvenient."

Sabrina begins to fret that Emily will decline and keeps her fingers crossed when she adds, "I take off from a different area from all the rest, and I'll give you a flight that you will never forget. You won't find a better deal. Believe me, this will be a day like no other in your life."

There is a short hesitation before Emily agrees. She takes down the pickup instructions and hangs up. Emily is excited with anticipation and has a restless night thinking about the invigorating trip she will have in the morning. Regan is less enthused and not sure about paragliding. He, too, has a restless night. He taps Emily. "As long as we are both restless and not sleeping, we might as well have some fun." With that, he caresses her belly, and the fun begins.

At eight o'clock the following morning, Emily is picked up by Sabrina in front of the hotel. "Hello, Emily, I'm Kelly. Are you ready for a magical, fun, and unforgettable morning?" she asks.

"I am a little nervous and not a great fan of heights, but you might call me an adrenaline junkie. I like to live a bit dangerously," Emily replies. Sabrina sees the shimmering red around her face, the sign of a human unworthy of life.

They take off in a jeep and drive the steep mountain roads, lined with furry Highland cows with their bells, casually watching them pass by. Emily sees the clear blue of the lakes and the river that coils through the landscape. A blue she has never seen before. Spectacular. The day is getting off to a good start.

When they arrive at the takeoff point, Sabrina begins to lay out the paragliding equipment and the helmets. She soon secures Emily in the leather seat and is poised to get in behind her. Emily cannot see that Sabrina is not strapping herself into the leather seat that connects Emily to "Kelly." Sabrina was never going to be a part of this ride.

"Are we all set, Kelly? What do we do now? I am so nervous," Emily says with a tremble in her voice.

Little does she know she has ten minutes to live.

"Emily, you are secured in your seat. Hand me your phone, or you will lose it. Almost everyone drops their phone. I will be taking the pictures with an extendable selfie stick. I'll give you a thumb drive when we land. Now we are going to run down this sloping grass field until the parachute expands, then we will be up and off. Hold on to the right and left guides with me. Ready? Here we go."

Sabrina gets behind Emily, and they both run down the sloped grass field until the parachute fills with air and then lifts off. With a huge push, Emily is off.

The ground has fallen away, and she is high over the meadows. The view is breathtaking, and for a minute, soaring like an eagle, Emily is the happiest she has ever been. "Kelly, this is exhilarating. We are so high up . . . Kelly? Kelly?"

Emily looks back, but Kelly is not there. She is by herself. What the hell? She looks around, but already she can't see where she took off from. But then she hears a voice, shouting, "This is for ripping off all the children that you are supposed to be helping."

Panic sets in. First, a panic that she's been found out. *Who the hell is Kelly anyway?* But then the panic of her immediate situation hits her. She was relying on Kelly on this flight. *What do I do? How does this steer?*

Emily is truly scared. She is so high. Her brain isn't functioning properly amid all the panic. She's frozen. *Is this how it ends? Oh Lord.* She begins to tremble, first her hands, then her arms, then her whole body. The parachute begins to soar higher in the updraft, but the flight is becoming unstable, and it twists and turns. Emily can't control this parachute. She pulls left, then right, hoping to steady the paraglider, but it makes it worse. She begins screaming for help, but no one can help her. She is flying alone guided only by the mercy of the wind. She has no control. She is so high above the ground. All she can do is stop struggling and hope that she'll make it back to land somehow. But soon she sees she is headed for a mountainside, a sheer rock face, and the wind seems to be carrying her toward it faster and faster.

Sabrina is watching the small dot of the paraglider. She smiles when Emily is carried by the wind currents toward it. There has always been a tiny chance that Emily might survive this flight, which was a concern, but now it seems the plan is working. Emily is in serious, deadly trouble.

Sabrina's dark passenger is coming alive; the secret place where her demon sleeps is now a place of excitement. Death is near. The taste is close. The thirst for death is about to be quenched.

Emily sees the mountain granite coming closer. She is heading toward the rock, so high up. She is going to hit the rock mountain at a very fast rate. She knows there is no escape. She is crying.

A distant scream is heard. A final scream.

Later that day, Jason Dempsey is on the runway with only Regan as his passenger.

"Where is Emily?" Jason asks Regan.

Regan responds slowly and with tears in his eyes, "Emily went paragliding, and apparently something went wrong. She crashed into a mountain and was killed. Her guide was not found, and Emily is so far up the mountain that it will take several days for a team of climbers to get to her body. I was waiting for her to return. I was going to go paragliding next. I was nervous, and now I know why. It's freakin' dangerous. Why does your company arrange discounts for such dangerous activities?"

Jason is shocked and confused. What is Regan talking about? His company doesn't partner with activity providers . . . but that thought is soon displaced. For some reason, Jason feels alive at the thought of Emily dying. She was on the take from her nonprofit that she led. He told Frank about her, hoping that he might pass on information to the police, but this makes him happy. He is elated. He feels something inside him is invigorated.

He looks in his mirror and sees that he is red. He wipes the mirror, but it's not the glass. This confuses him too. He often sees his wife, Kari, red, and lately he is noticing his son Nelson is taking on a red tinge. What does this mean? Why was he thrilled when Regan talked of the death of Emily?

Jason turns his jet to the runway and is given permission to depart. Off into the wild blue yonder he flies. Regan only requires water from the flight attendant, so her workload on the trip home is minimal. After he lands and his passenger and flight attendant leave the jet, Jason departs.

At home, he tells Kari about his passenger who has died in a freak accident while paragliding. Of course, Kari knew what was going to happen to Emily Carson, but she listens intently to Jason and is thrilled to see him glowing red.

As he tells Kari the story, he again begins to feel thrilled, his heart is beating faster, and something in him is pleased. He holds his hands up in front of him and sees that they are red. He looks questioningly at Kari, but she, too, is red and seems to be excited about hearing of Emily's gruesome death. She seems electrified too.

"Kari, what is going on? Why am I excited about this death? Why am I red? Why are you red?" pleads Jason.

"Tell me your deepest secret, Jason, something you have never told anyone, something that scares you," says Kari.

Jason holds Kari's hand and looks down as he says, "Kari, for as long as I can remember, I have always wanted to kill someone. And something in my chest wants that kill, needs that kill, demands that kill. What's wrong with me?"

Kari is shocked but also comforted. She knew Jason was special, but she cannot believe that Jason is just like her. Kari cannot believe that someone unrelated to her family has the gift. It is so enlightening to discover that other families in this world have the desire to kill and have the monster in them. Kari is shocked but happy to share this with her life partner.

She tells Jason about the Emily Carson plan and Sabrina's role. Jason listens, his jaw open. She concludes, "Jason, you are a part of something special. Only a few members of our family have this gift that you are describing. We work together, and we work silently. This is a gift that must never be discussed outside of our very small ring. I will be meeting with my father and Sabrina shortly, and I want you to be there with me. They will be shocked that someone outside of our immediate family has the gift." She hugs him and can feel his electricity. And he can feel hers.

Kari thinks, *I hope Frank and Sabrina will be pleased.*

†

CHAPTER 11

FRANK, SABRINA, AND KARI are meeting in Frank's office. Jason is waiting in the living room.

Frank says, "Kari, why did you bring Jason to our private meeting? Is something wrong? Is there something we need to know?"

Kari says with pride, "I've got something exciting to tell you. I believe that Jason has the gift."

Frank's and Sabrina's eyebrows lift in unison, but Kari sees some concern in their eyes.

Kari continues. "I know. It's incredible. But truly, when he learned of Emily's death, something came over him, something he could not control, something he could not explain. And now he is showing up red. Not as strongly as us, no, but when we talked about death, the red grew stronger. I asked him to tell me his deepest secret, and he told me of his strong desire to kill. That confused him, and he wanted to know why he was red and why he saw both me and Nelson as red."

Frank says, "His red is not strong. I didn't see it on him just now, but he is one of us and has the gift, and it is nurtured. It will grow stronger in time."

Sabrina is completely stunned. Someone from a completely different bloodline has the gift? Unheard of. They have always wondered if other families have the special gift. They've often wondered if they are the only family in the world with this need to kill. And here is their answer. *No*, there are others.

Frank regains his composure and invites Jason in to join them. He says, "Kari, thank you for bringing Jason to us." Then Frank looks at Jason. "Jason, you have just answered a question we have long wondered. My question to you is, are you one of a long family line, or are you the first in your family to have this gift?"

Jason thinks for a moment. "Frank, my parents never talked about killing. I am an only child, but I never heard my other relatives talk of killing either. I never saw any red in my family."

Frank says, "Then you are the first in your bloodline."

Kari then says, "Dad, we think Nelson, our son, also has the gift. We have noticed that he has a faint red swirl about him. We will continue to watch him, but the signs are there."

"Well," says Frank, "this meeting sure turned out differently than I expected. But perhaps the timing of this information is fitting. I brought you here to tell you that I'm going to stop participating in the kills. I am getting too old, and, unlike with my father, my inner demon can be controlled. The future kills you provide will satisfy my monster." Frank has not told them about killing Bernard Baker. This was Frank's kill, and they would have talked him out of it. They are beginning to distrust Frank, and he knows it.

"I will take a mentor role, and the three of you can continue. We can still meet here, and we can all help to train Jason and teach him the ways of our life. Jason, we are glad to welcome you to our family business."

Sabrina says, "While we are here, I want to go back to our discussion about Sergio Martinez, the diamond thief. Jason, this will be a good introduction to our family business."

Jason's red aura surges for a moment, and he leans in, eager to begin right away in the family business.

Sabrina continues and explains to Jason what she told the other two before: that Sergio Martinez sells diamond jewelry to wealthy, older clients for cash, then arranges robberies to recover the goods, which he then resells. Over and over again. With the profits from this lucrative moneymaking scheme, he trades weapons to militias, guerillas, gangs, and mafiosos in other countries. He is the cause of much death and destruction and human misery in these places.

She says, "He operates in plain view and thinks he is untouchable. We are about to show him that it is a fallacy. He is a person to eliminate. I have formulated a plan, and I'm currently looking for a helicopter to aid in our removal of this miserable person. Can you help, Jason?"

Jason perks up. "I have access to the new Bell 505 Jet Ranger X helicopter that seats five. I also am trained to pilot this helicopter. Let me know a few days in advance, and I can have this helicopter available."

Frank, Sabrina, and Kari look at each other, then at Jason.

"You seem to be starting quickly," says Frank.

Kari is beaming, and Jason is proud to be a part of this kill team.

Frank says, "Actually, I know what I said, but I want to be a part of this kill for the last time before I retire from the family business." He feels this mission will be safe because Sabrina's in charge, and he cannot put them at risk.

Sabrina and Kari smile knowingly. "Of course, Dad," says Kari.

One week later, Sergio Martinez has his diamond display case open and is showing his latest client, Barbara Sinclair, his diamond rings, bracelets, and necklaces. "This is the finest diamond jewelry money can buy. Look at the exquisite craftsmanship in each piece," says Sergio to Sabrina. Sabrina is posing as a wealthy client, Barbara Sinclair.

Sabrina says, "My husband, Rafael, will be here in a moment, and I am sure he will want me to have many of your beautiful pieces." Sabrina has told Sergio that Mr. Sinclair is a philanthropist who never courts publicity. Right on cue, Frank James can be heard entering the house. A moment later, he enters the room.

"Hello, you must be Sergio," Frank says, putting his hand out to Sergio in greeting. Sergio shakes his hand. Frank says, "I am Rafael Sinclair. It looks as if Barbara has chosen some jewelry from your selection."

"She has indeed, sir. Let me show you this one piece that would be perfect." As Sergio is focused on selecting a beautiful ring, Frank stabs Sergio's neck with a syringe of brown liquid that renders him immobile within a few seconds, and he drops to the finely carpeted floor, staring up at Frank in confusion. *What the hell is happening? Am I being robbed?* are his thoughts. *Rafael and Barbara Sinclair, you have messed with the wrong person. If you only knew me. You are dead. As soon as I get out of this, I'm coming back with my boys, and you will die,* he thinks. He wants to say the words, but they will not come out of his frozen mouth. Sergio's body has betrayed him. The brown liquid has left his eyes and mind working but nothing else.

Frank looks Sergio square in the eyes and says, "Sergio, you must think we are robbing you, and you would be partly right. We will be taking your diamonds and your cash, but these assets will be used to help others in the community, a nonprofit called Children's Life, to be specific. Your fraudulent career stops today, here and now."

Sabrina steps forward into Sergio's line of sight. "Your life stops today too. While we don't like your stealing, the main reason you're here, under our control, is that we know about your arms deals, selling weapons to renegades around the world, not caring about who gets harmed and killed. Many innocent men, women, and children die because of your disregard for life. We are going to take you for a little helicopter ride that you will never forget."

Sergio's mind is turning. *Who are these people, and how do they know my business? They don't look like killers*, he thinks, which is a thought that comforts him. Surely they won't actually kill him; they're just trying to scare him into giving up his bad ways. He will give them up, or will tell them so, when he can speak again . . . but he won't give them up for long.

Frank and Sabrina struggle with Sergio's limp body as they take him outside to a waiting car on the drive, careful that nobody spots them, and off to the airport they go. Sabrina has put handcuffs on Sergio, but they are useless for a body that does not work, but the handcuffs are on for a special reason that Sergio will soon learn.

On the Jet Center apron, Frank and Jason bustle Sergio onto the Bell helicopter and secure his seat belt. Jason gets into the pilot's seat and starts up the Bell 505 with Frank, Sabrina, and Kari—the rest of the kill team—aboard.

As they are flying toward the vast ocean, Kari is fooling around with Sergio's handcuffs. He is totally distracted, not noticing what Kari is doing. He's too busy thinking, *Where are they taking me? They must want a ransom. They are all dead when I get out of this. All of them.* But small beads of sweat are accumulating on his forehead and going down his neck. His whole body is damp with sweat, but his mouth is going dry.

Soon Jason has them out over a pitch-black ocean on a moonless night. The chopper slows down and lowers the elevation until it is only forty feet above the ocean.

Frank looks at Sergio Martinez and says, "This is the end of the line for you. No more robbery, no more weapons, no more lives lost."

Sergio's breathing is accelerated, his eyes are wide open, and he is in panic mode. He looks down at his handcuffed hands and sees that Kari has attached a chain with an anchor.

Sergio has three minutes to live.

Dread fills Sergio. He feels the heavy, cold hand of death upon him.

He cannot struggle. He cannot talk. *What a terrible way to die. Help me,* his eyes plead. His body has betrayed him. He cannot move, wiggle, or even scream, which he is doing inside his head.

As Jason keeps the helicopter steady, Frank opens the Bell helicopter door, and everyone looks at the inky black water below. Sergio can't believe that he is in this situation. He knows he is about to die. A small tear escapes his right eye.

He is shoved hard from his warm seat out into the cold. He falls through the air for forty feet and then hits the bitter cold water hard.

The anchor pulls him down into the dark abyss.

He is alone, in the black, in the cold, farther and farther from the world of the living, deeper and deeper toward oblivion.

†

CHAPTER 12

JASON IS NOW OFFICIALLY part of the family kill team. For the first time in his life, he feels his family understands him. His family by marriage. All those years of questioning himself, all the years he felt alone and did not understand his urges, are now clear to him. He has tried to fit into his peer group, but no one he knew thought murder was acceptable. He always felt like an outsider, alone with his thoughts. To be in a family where the gift is accepted and embraced is exciting. With them, death is not a foe but a friend. Jason is ready to embrace it, to feel its power. He is open to learning and living his life with his inner monster. Jason is ready.

Kari has a case coming into her law office that she does not work on but is interested in. It involves Jackson Garwood, who is on trial for domestic abuse of his partner, Donna Cup, and her daughter, Leslie Cup. It was a vicious cycle. He beat Donna, then said he was sorry, and she took him back. It happened again when Jackson was drinking and thought Donna was making too much noise, so he beat her until she was quiet. But the neighbors knew that Jackson was a problem and called the police to protect Donna and her daughter. One day, the police rushed to her home and, after looking at the damage done to Donna, arrested Jackson. He was charged with domestic abuse, but through a technicality he only got a six-month jail term.

Kari tells this story to Sabrina and Jason. "I think we need to get involved. Jackson has a long history of domestic violence. He has a pattern of behavior in all his relationships. Any woman who comes in contact with him is in jeopardy of damage by Jackson." Frank and Sabrina agree and decide to intervene. Jackson Garwood is not going to get away with this. Jackson's color is deep red, so he is a candidate for justice.

Sabrina tells Jason, "I know that Jackson will not change his abusive ways, and Donna and Leslie will be in danger when Jackson gets out of jail, especially when he discovers what happened while he's been inside."

Jason looks confused. "And what's that?"

"She won the lottery! Can you believe it? $10 million!"

Jason laughs. "Good for her. Divine compensation for all her trauma."

"But when he gets out and sees how well she's doing, it'll make him mad, I reckon," says Sabrina. "We need to take him down."

Jason agrees it is time to give Jackson some of what he was dishing out. "He is a bully to women," Jason says. "I will be ready when Jackson returns." Jason has a double shot of the family's amazing brown liquid at the ready.

But Jason is nervous. He thinks, *Jackson is not a small guy, and after six months in prison, he'll be even bigger and angrier. He'll have learned some new violent tricks inside.* But Jason is keen to prove himself, so he keeps his worries to himself.

Sabrina visits Donna at home, posing as a parole officer, and tells her, "We know the kind of man Jackson is, and we are here to help you. When Jackson gets out of jail, he may come here. I will arrange for someone to protect you. He may need to contain Jackson and will use whatever means necessary to restrain him and protect you and your daughter. Here is my number. Do not hesitate to call."

Donna keeps the card and tells Sabrina, "I'm sure Jackson is sorry for what he did and will have learned his lesson by going to jail. I think we will be fine, but I will keep your card just in case. Thank you."

Just as Sabrina predicted, it doesn't take Jackson long after his release to find out about his ex-partner's good fortune. After she landed him in prison, this makes him furious. He knows he can't go within half a mile of her, by order of the court, but his anger drives him. He disguises himself well and finds the house where Donna and Leslie have been living. It is a luxurious place. And there he's been, in a tiny cell with another maniac for six months who liked to fight him every night.

He marches up to the front door and rings the bell. Then he hammers on the door.

Upstairs, Donna can see a man. Despite his disguise, she knows exactly who it is. His fury is palpable, and she won't risk another lengthy stay in the hospital. These past six months, she has realized how toxic and dangerous he is. Enough is enough.

She calls Sabrina. "Hi, this is Donna. Jackson is here, and he looks mad as hell. Please help us."

Sabrina replies, "Jason will be there right away."

Jason gets the call from Sabrina, and he springs into action. He is prepared mentally and physically. But thoughts creep into his mind. *What if Jackson overpowers me?* Jason tries to overcome these doubts with, *You will be fine; you are strong and capable.*

Jason goes to the house and is ready. His inner demon, his dark passenger, is ready. Jackson is pacing outside the house, hoping Donna will relent and let him in. Jason approaches him from behind, and when he's close enough, he leaps toward Jackson and tries to push the needle of the vial of brown liquid into Jackson's neck, but Jackson pushes Jason and his needle away.

"Who the hell are you?" Jackson yells.

"You're violating the terms of your release," says Jason as calmly as he can.

"I'm not going back to prison." Jackson spits and goes for Jason.

Jason is surprised by Jackson's strength and ability. Jason struggles to get the upper hand, and all of a sudden, he finds himself trapped beneath Jackson. Jason struggles to get Jackson off of him. It's then he sees Kari with the needle in her hand and Donna and Leslie behind her, holding each other. He rolls Jackson off him. "Wow, great timing. I was having a bit of trouble with this big hunk," says Jason.

Kari smiles at him. "So I see."

Jason gets to his feet and dusts himself off.

Kari turns to Donna and Leslie and says, "I knew Jason was coming here to help you two, but I was worried."

"And you're from law enforcement too?" Donna asks. She looks terrified and is struggling to understand.

"I am," Kari says. "We had the house under surveillance because we know the offender is dangerous. Good thing we did."

"Now what?" Leslie asks, half hidden behind her mother.

"I'm calling 911. He'll be taken to Kensington Hospital," says Kari. "You're safe now. He won't bother you anymore."

"Will they take him back to prison when he's out of the hospital?" Donna asks.

Kari nods, but she knows he won't be leaving the hospital.

After three days in the hospital, Frank, posing as a doctor, sits with Donna and Leslie and says, "Jackson has suffered a hemorrhagic stroke. This will leave him without the ability to talk, walk, or even breathe on his own. He has named you as his next of kin, and we know he has no other relatives. So, I'm sorry to say that you will need to decide if we withdraw life support."

Donna and Leslie feel some compassion for Jackson but remember the beatings, so that compassion quickly goes away. Donna and Leslie fill out fake paperwork for Jackson's death.

As she signs, Donna thinks, *Jackson is not a relative, and I am not spending all my money keeping Jackson on life support*. This seems fair to all except Jackson, who still understands what's going on. *Who is this doctor who's telling them lies?* His lights are on; he's not as good as dead, but now he's going to die with Donna's permission? She is killing him, and there's nothing he can do about it.

After Donna and Leslie kiss him on the forehead, they leave the hospital room.

Jackson Greenwood has only an hour left to live.

Jason enters the room and approaches the bed. He leans over and says, "Jackson Garwood, your days of domestic abuse are over. You will die at the hands of the woman you abused. But just so you know, you have made me very happy. I am able to kill you, and my future life with my family starts with you. Thank you."

Jason's inner monster is elated as he removes the pillow from behind Jackson's head and places it over his face. Frank is outside, ensuring Jason is not disturbed. Without a struggle, it is hard to know if Jackson is dead, but Jason feels the moment of his death as a thrill in his own soul. He senses something inside of himself, a deep satisfaction and electric joy that tells him his first kill is complete.

From that point on, life is good for Donna and Leslie.

CHAPTER 13

FRANK, SABRINA, KARI, AND JASON are discussing the Jackson Garwood case, and everyone is excited. The room full of inner monsters is pleased. "Monsters" because they can be terrifying and aggressive to those they are up against but protectors for those they reside within.

Jason has done a good job under pressure and against a bigger, stronger man. And a big thanks to Kari for helping out when Jason really needed some help. Jackson Garwood will no longer be a threat to Donna or Leslie or the community as a whole. And that makes all the demons happy.

The family feels they are doing a good job and ridding society of bad people. They feel safe.

They are wrong.

Something is happening as they sit in their warm office praising themselves. Something that will turn Sabrina's world upside down.

The phone rings. Sam Jefferson, Sabrina's husband, is on the phone. "Sabrina," he says with fear in his voice, "Lyndsey is missing. She was supposed to be home at two. It's now five, and I can't get hold of her. I've called her friends, her work, and now you."

Sabrina is concerned but keeps her cool. "I'm sure it's fine, Sam. Teenagers live in their own little worlds. She's probably somewhere, maybe with a guy we don't know about. I don't think the police will take us seriously after only three hours. Let's keep trying her cell."

Sam reluctantly agrees and hangs up. But Sabrina can't help but worry. Children are always a worry, especially in their family, with its connections to the worst people in society. What if someone has found out about the family business and wants revenge?

"Go home and wait," says Frank. "Keep me in the loop. I can ask my contacts at the police department to keep an eye and ear out for anything that might be relevant to us, informally, of course. I'll let you know if I hear something."

Sabrina tries to think positively as she drives home to Sam. *It'll be fine*, she thinks. *Just some teenage hijinks.* But she has been home less than an hour when the phone rings. It is police officer Martin: "Mrs. Jefferson, we just got information about a sighting of Lyndsey. It's not good news, I'm afraid. Someone reported seeing a young woman being thrown into a dark blue van over on Twelfth Street. Cameras in the area picked up the incident, and the woman matches the description Frank gave of her. We are searching the area for a dark blue van and any leads. We will keep in touch. A team of officers is on their way over to fill you in as this proceeds."

Sabrina cannot speak. She hangs up and tries to convey the conversation to Sam. Sam and Sabrina are home together, wondering how a thing like this could happen.

Lyndsey is afraid.

A man asked her for directions as she was walking down the street, but as soon as she started talking, he reached across and hit her on the side of her head. For a moment she blacked out. He got out of his van and pushed her roughly inside the dirty van. He quickly tied her up and sped away. When she awoke, she was woozy, and her head hurt. The ropes on her arms and legs were too tight and cut into her skin.

Now she is in a dimly lit room. Lyndsey pretends to still be unconscious as she sneaks a look at the man to try and remember whatever she can so that she can identify the man if she can get away from him. He is sitting in the corner of the room, absorbed by his phone. He is a big guy, maybe six feet, with greasy brown hair and black, heavy-rimmed glasses. Maybe in his midthirties. A large tattoo of a seminaked girl on his left arm and a scattering of random tattoos on his right arm and neck. Then she looks around the basement room. There are some high windows, blacked out, and the walls have been soundproofed. She realizes that this is not his first time kidnapping someone. She is lying in a single bed. There is a toilet across the room and nothing else.

Her wrists and legs are in pain from the harsh rope keeping her tied up, and she shifts to find more comfort. Her movement attracts his attention. "Don't move. Don't do nothing till I tell ya to!" he yells at her.

"Can you loosen these ties?" Lyndsey says, tears in her eyes.

"Only speak when I tell you to!" he shouts.

He jumps up and is beside her in an instant. He smacks her once, hard, to show his intentions are real. He leaves her in the room with the door closed for two long hours. She is terrified. All she can do is try to sleep and block out this living nightmare.

Later, she hears him coming down the stairs. The man comes in and finally unties her. She rubs her wrists and legs to get the circulation working and tries rubbing the pain away.

He says, "My name is Daniel Oscar Allen. Remember that, and only call me by that name. Got it? Daniel Oscar Allen." She nods her head in compliance. He leaves, slamming the door behind him.

Lyndsey is frightened but keeps his name in her thoughts. "I'll call you Daniel Oscar Allen, but I am going to get out of here," she whispers. Lyndsey knows she will have to get out of this on her own. No one would know to look for her here. Hopefully, they will have some information on Daniel Oscar Allen, if he has been caught before or has an arrest record. But all this is hopeful thinking. Lyndsey is on her own and knows it. She will have to save herself. She looks around to see if she has any resources and sees a seam in the padded wall. Maybe there is something there? She keeps assessing the room closely until she hears him coming down the stairs.

Daniel Oscar Allen unlocks the door and enters. "I guess you want to know why you are here. What are my intentions, and if you might escape?" says Daniel. "You are here for my pleasure, to do what I want with. When I want something from you, you obey. If you do, there is a chance I will set you free. If not, I will punish you, and you'll never see the outside again. You will never see your family and friends again. Got that?" He leaves the room with a slam of the door.

Something inside Lyndsey begins to stir. Something she is unfamiliar with.

An hour later, Daniel comes back and opens the door. Daniel is there with a sandwich and carton of juice. "Eat up. You are going to need your strength. I'll be back, and you're going to be my dessert tonight."

He slams the door when he leaves. Shaking, Lyndsey eats the food. She will need her strength to fight him off. She again sobs in her pillow, but now as she lies there, she begins to feel something. It is deep inside her chest. But there is nothing in her small room to defend herself with.

What am I going to do when he comes in again? Lyndsey knows she must come up with a plan. He will be back, and soon. She visualizes hurting him, killing him, and when she does, something stirs within her. Something deep in her. Something ancient, yet something new. Something with a need. She is suddenly energized. She imagines different scenarios over and over of killing him, and the feeling inside grows so strong that she is sure she can kill him, or at least incapacitate him.

Sure enough, soon his footsteps can be heard approaching.

He goes directly for Lyndsey, aggressively, saying, "Calm down and do as I say and as I want. Do not resist."

But she pushes him with all her might. He struggles with her. The fight is on. It should not be a fair fight, but Lyndsey's newfound strength takes them both by surprise. Suddenly, he slaps her hard with his meaty palm. Lyndsey falls back on the bed. Lyndsey thinks, *Someone help me, rescue me, save me.* Lyndsey is panicked, but then she pictures his dead body, and a calm comes over her. A deep calm when she should not be calm at all. Something has taken over her. The fear has gone. With an ear-piercing screech, she swings her fist at his head and strikes him hard. He falls back, stunned, a look of fear in his eyes. Who is this supernatural creature he's kidnapped? He stumbles to his feet, breathing hard, trying to decide if he can overcome her. With a growl, he blunders out of the room again.

Alone again, something both unfamiliar and comforting begins to happen. She looks at her hands, and they seem to be glowing red. The fist she used to hit him is not broken or even bruised. She flexes her fingers: there is no pain. Something is stirring inside her. Something that feels powerful. Something that desires contact with Daniel.

The next morning, around ten o'clock, the door opens, and Daniel brings her breakfast. He sets it down without saying anything and leaves. Clearly her outburst has shaken his confidence. Lyndsey eats, then sits on the bed, waiting, hoping he'll return so that she can kill him. All night she has lain awake thinking of doing so, feeling more alive in this bunker than she has ever felt. Something sleeping is awakening. Lyndsey can feel a thrill travel through her body. She is not afraid but waiting. She is not sure for what, but she is totally alive and buzzing when the door opens. She feels a strength that is unfamiliar, a confidence that is not unsure but determined. She is ready and willing to engage.

Daniel opens the door. He looks drunk or high and furious. He's obviously been trying to work up to this. She laughs at him.

"You're pathetic, Daniel Oscar Allen," she jeers. She stands facing him, feeling ten feet tall, every nerve electrified.

Daniel feels a change in Lyndsey. Lyndsey seems unafraid and even ready to defend herself.

Daniel has forty-five minutes to live.

Daniel says, "Don't fight me; just let this happen. There is nothing you can do. I outweigh you by a hundred and thirty pounds. You are no match for me. Do you understand?"

"Yes, Daniel Oscar Allen, I hear you, but you are wrong on two points. One, I will fight you, and two, there is something I can do," Lyndsey says calmly.

Daniel stares at Lyndsey, but the thing Lyndsey has been feeling inside now bubbles with inhuman strength; the red demon is ready. The fury that has been building in Lyndsey is at a boiling point.

Lyndsey says, "You have made a serious mistake kidnapping me and thinking you can do whatever you want to me." Lyndsey is unsure where these words are coming from, but she is confident and determined that this will be a fight.

Daniel hesitates for a second. "I will do real damage to you. You asked for this."

Lyndsey says, "You are not going to destroy me. In fact, I am going to take your life from you."

With that, Daniel leaps at Lyndsey, but the thing Lyndsey has been feeling inside now erupts, and with inhuman strength, the red demon lets loose. The inner monster that the family bloodline has inherited explodes and scratches, beats, and pounds Daniel Oscar Allen.

Lyndsey has unleashed the inner monster she never knew she had. Her strength is beyond her imagination. The fury is too much for Daniel. He is horrified that he is being beaten. He is alarmed that this little girl possesses so much anger and aggressive strength. Daniel is hurt and hurt badly. Lacerations cover his face. Lyndsey has hit him with a solid wooden stick she pried from the wall she found behind that seam in the padding.

Daniel is bleeding, gasping for air, and battered. He lifts himself onto his left elbow, leaning, but that arm is weak, and he falls to the ground. He looks at Lyndsey with bloodshot eyes, wondering how she beat him this way.

Lyndsey is excited beyond belief. She is invigorated, not tired from the combat. She says to Daniel, "You're a bad man. This room tells me you have done this before. How many times? Plenty, I bet. But you made a mistake with me. I have something inside me that was just waiting for someone like you. Someone to push me too far. To threaten me. To try and take my life. This is your last time."

Daniel is near death.

Lyndsey senses that this thing inside her is there to protect her, whatever it may be. She is not sure she is the same person that was kidnapped two days ago. Lyndsey feels powerful, invigorated. Just when she needed it, a quiet rage came alive.

She grabs Daniel, still surprised at her strength, and lifts him like a sack of potatoes, carrying him up the stairs. She gets him into his own van, closes the doors, starts up, and drives him to the Kensington police station. She goes into the police station to report that she is freed from this monster and that he is in serious condition in the back of the van. His own van.

The officer asks, "Do you know his name?"

Lyndsey says, "Yes, this is Daniel Oscar Allen."

Or rather, he *was* Daniel Oscar Allen. By the time the cops get a look at him, he's dead. Lyndsey stands by while an officer declares him dead on arrival. *Daniel Oscar Allen, DOA, is dead on arrival!* Lyndsey cannot suppress a grin at Daniel's expense.

The police officer looks at Lyndsey, then looks at Daniel. The officer asks, "How could you take on a man like Daniel and win? What really happened? Are you telling us the truth?"

Lyndsey smiles and says, "He may have been large, but he was nothing but a small, pathetic man." She wants to tell them that she had help from an inner strength, something she never knew she had. But they would not understand . . . *She* doesn't even understand it, not yet.

The police are amazed. They tell her she will have to make a statement, but from where they stand, it appears to be a simple case of self-defense, and then they drive her to the hospital to be examined.

Her inner monster has introduced herself in a most unusual way. Lyndsey feels empowered. Energy is spinning throughout her body. The monster is pleased. Lyndsey is pleased.

Daniel Oscar Allen is where he should be.

Lyndsey calls her mom from the police station to tell her she is okay, but she hints that there's something more she wants to say. "Mom, what a story I have for you. Love you." Sabrina is surprised to hear her daughter sounding so elated after such a terrible ordeal. Is she tired? Yes. Exhausted? Yes, but fully alert, fully present, and full of unbridled energy. Lyndsey is alive and can feel every particle of her being.

Across town, Sabrina is shaking with happiness at the news her daughter is safe at the hospital. She calls the family and lets them know Lyndsey has escaped and appears to be uninjured, although she has not yet been examined. Sabrina, Sam, and their other daughter, Tiffany Rose, go right to Kensington Hospital. They all hug her and celebrate her escape from her near-death ordeal at the hands of Daniel Oscar Allen. Sabrina is angry that her daughter went through a harrowing experience and thinks that it's a good thing DOA was, indeed, dead already. She hugs Lyndsey and does not want to let go. After Lyndsey is examined at the hospital, Sabrina and Sam take her home, the place where she belongs. Where she is loved.

At home, Sabrina is curious about how her daughter overpowered a full-grown man with bad intentions. Lyndsey begins to tell her tale in detail. When she starts to talk about an inner strength, something protective, Sabrina is alarmed. Can this experience have triggered the gift in Lyndsey? She doesn't appear to be red at all. But maybe it comes out when she is in danger or made angry enough. Now is not the time to explore the possibilities; Lyndsey must rest.

Sabrina says, "Lyndsey, you must be exhausted. Why don't you take a shower, lie down, and we will talk in more depth later?"

Lyndsey leaves to clean up and rest up, and Sabrina ponders her next move. She will tell Sam and Tiffany Rose a cleaned-up version once she learns of Lyndsey's full ordeal and try to make it more plausible that she overcame her kidnapper. Sabrina suspects something incredible has happened but is unsure what. Lyndsey has never shown any red coloring; her daughter was a typical young teenager until yesterday. Today she has come home changed.

The next day, when Lyndsey is rested, she sits with her mom and tells her the full tale. When she is done with the facts, she pauses. Lyndsey continues, "It was so weird, Mom. Every time I thought about killing him, I was filled with a sense of great power. This great power inside of me roared to the surface, and as I was being attacked, this thing inside me took over, and I attacked him without mercy, without feelings, without fear. I had the strength to carry him up the stairs and into his van and calmly drove him to the police station. How was that possible?"

Sabrina says, "Lyndsey, you have been through a harrowing experience. I want you to sit down with your Uncle Frank and cousins Kari and Jason tomorrow, and let's discuss this. There is much to tell you, and there is much you can teach us."

Lyndsey says, "Mom, what is going on? Why do I need to sit down with Frank, Kari, and Jason?"

Sabrina says, "Let's wait for tomorrow. All will be explained."

The next day at Frank's office, Frank, Sabrina, Kari, and Jason listen to Lyndsey's story with fascination.

Lyndsey says, "Whatever happened to me was lifesaving. I felt invincible in a situation where I should have been hurt very seriously."

Sabrina tells Lyndsey, "Lyndsey, the four of us have a family secret that we want to tell you about. There is a gift that a small fraction of our family is honored with."

Between them, they explain it all to Lyndsey as clearly as possible, mindful of not frightening her. It's not easy to explain how they as a group are eliminating red people that need to be dealt with, but Lyndsey is taking it all in. Sabrina continues, "For us, it is a powerful gift that lets us kill without guilt or fear and with the blessing from a power bigger than us. Lyndsey, your situation was unique in the family history. We have never had a situation where the inner monster came out of nowhere to protect a family member. It looked out for you and would not let you be killed."

Lyndsey says, "But what does it mean?"

Frank says, "We can't be sure, so we must simply keep an eye on things. You may not have the desire to kill unless you're in immediate danger."

Sabrina continues, "The monster refused to show itself except when imminent death was trying to take you. It would not let that happen. This is new to us. We are amazed and truly shocked by what happened to you. We always thought the monster needed a kill to be satisfied, that it was a beast demanding us to kill, but you have shown us the monster also needs to protect us."

Everyone is overjoyed by the discovery.

CHAPTER 14

FRANK JAMES IS NEARING the last years of his life. He has had an outstanding career as a police detective and a long marriage to his wonderful wife, Carla, who passed away years earlier. Frank is adrift without his Carla. She was his anchor, his everything. She never knew of his other life of death and killing. She had suspected something was up with Frank, but he made sure to keep her insulated from that life.

The family now has six members with the gift. Frank, Sabrina, Kari, Jason, Nelson, and now Sabrina's daughter, Lyndsey.

One day, Kari says to Sabrina and Jason, "Dad is fading, and he knows it. His time is coming to an end. He is still interested in the family business, but his passion is fading. The family members with the gift need to keep a close eye on him. He's still important to the family and much respected and loved."

Sabrina continues, "Soon I will be the new leader of the family business. Do we believe there are other families out there with the gift? The family is learning. There are other bloodlines out there that can expand the family, like Jason, and now it seems the gift has different priorities for different people, like Lyndsey. And we've learned that the inner demons enjoy suicides as well as killings. Maybe this is new, or maybe we're learning. Perhaps this gift is evolving. Time will tell."

A few weeks later, during a family meeting, Jason introduces a new target to the team. He has been watching a celebrity, Peter Owens, who occasionally uses Jason's private jet services when flying abroad. Jason says, "He is a C-list celebrity, but don't tell him that. He walks and talks like the most famous celebrity. He had a walk-on part in a big fantasy TV series, but you would think he was the hero the way he talks about it."

Sabrina looks at an image of the actor on her phone and replies, "I think I know what you are talking about—a lot of swagger but not much to offer."

Jason laughs and says, "Peter Owens has hired me to fly him to a remote island in the Caribbean. Peter will be bringing Giana, his girlfriend—a famous model. She loves being important to a movie star, even though he would not be her first choice of movie star. My guess is that Giana thinks that being in the realm of movie stars will introduce her to more and better stars."

Kari chuckles. "How about I come with you as the flight attendant, and I can find out more about them?"

"Sounds great. It's a long trip, and I can use the company, especially yours," he says, looking lovingly at his beautiful wife. "The flight is tomorrow morning. We take off at ten."

The next day, at 9:30, the jet is warming up. Peter and Giana show up and climb aboard the smart jet. The doors lock, and at ten precisely, the jet begins to taxi along the runway and takes off for the Caribbean.

Jason and Kari notice Peter is as red as red can be and plan to find out why on this trip. Sabrina talks to Peter and Giana during the long flight and overhears their conversations. Peter is mean, selfish, and arrogant, but Giana is quiet, lovely, and easygoing. But Peter's redness must mean more.

Of course, it does. In fact, Peter is swindling everyone he knows. He's sold movie rights to movies he had no legal right to represent. He's talked friends, family, and strangers into investing in his schemes that would bear no ownership, profits, or even any chance of the movie being made. At one point in the flight, Peter says to Kari, "If you invest $10,000 in my company, I can guarantee you a return of $18,000 within six months. The shares are selling fast."

Kari, acting professionally, says, "Thank you, sir. That sounds good, but now is not a good time for me to invest."

Peter says, "Your loss."

But Peter knows his trip to an almost deserted island is more of an escape from people calling and demanding their money back than a vacation. Giana knows some of his history but not of his dire financial crisis. If she did, she would leave him in a heartbeat. He cannot allow that; she attracts much-needed attention by his side.

Jason gently lands the jet, and Kari is stunned at the remoteness of the island. Upon arrival at the lonely airstrip, no one is there to greet them, and the modest hotel is a dead giveaway that Peter is not a celebrity in this part of the world. But with his ill-gotten gains, he does have the best room in the hotel. There are no other guests, but that does not matter to Peter. The room is well-appointed and has ocean views. The hotel restaurant's food is excellent, but Giana quickly wishes she had not come on this trip. Peter had described the accommodations much differently. She is glad that Jason and Kari are staying at the hotel too, in case the couple wants to go island hopping, and she spends time with them in the bar while Peter is getting phone call after phone call. He answers a few of the calls, but his response is always the same: "Yes, yes, the money is on the way. You should have it within the week." Over and over, he spouts this lie, and his mood gets rougher and rougher. He begins yelling at Giana and anyone else he can find.

Jason sees an opportunity.

Jason tells Peter, "There is another island about an hour from here. You can't fly in, but there's a motorboat to use. Perhaps it's the ideal place for you to hide out for a few months until the heat dies down and your investors give up. They'll never find you there."

Peter ponders this, ignoring his ringing phone. "What about food and necessities that I will need?"

Jason says, "I have talked to Diego, a local who seems older than the islands themselves. He assures me that there is a small hut with solar power and clean water but not much else. I'll help you stock the small fridge-freezer. I'll see to it that you are resupplied regularly by the locals. That way you can stay here until you are safe to return without your friends and family wanting to get even with you. A time-out."

"Giana, you'll stay with me?" Peter asks.

Giana replies, "Not a chance, Peter, not a chance. I'm going back with Jason and Kari. I won't say a word to anyone about where you are or even where you might be, but I'm gone as soon as Jason's jet leaves."

Peter is worried, but he knows he is done for if he doesn't go off-grid. Hiding out is the best way to be safe and get out of the mess he's gotten into.

"Okay, Jason, let's go at the end of the week," says Peter.

Friday comes quickly, and Peter is nervous about being on a tiny island by himself. He says to Giana, "Come on, baby, stay with me. It'll be romantic being castaways!"

But Giana is firm in her decision. "No, Peter, you're on your own."

Peter says, "Will you wait for me? I don't know how long I'll be gone."

"Maybe," Giana says without any enthusiasm.

With supplies loaded on the boat driven by a local man with little English, Jason and Peter set off for the remote island. After an hour, they get to the island, unload, and get Peter into his new home—a small, dilapidated but usable hut in the wooded island with six large palm trees next to the small structure. The island is intoxicating with its clear blue water on all sides. There is no boat traffic, and no major airlines fly overhead.

"Home sweet home," Peter says when he is settled in. "I love it here; this will work perfectly as a retreat." Peter thinks, *No one will ever look for me here. I will be safe from prosecution and legal problems.*

Jason says goodbye and gets into the waiting boat. "Okay, Peter, a supply boat will visit every week, and when you want to leave, you can go back with the boatman."

Peter hesitates and says, "Okay." Now the time to be left alone is here. He's getting nervous. He laughs. "Don't forget about me. This island is so remote I'll never be found!"

With that, Jason gets back into the boat and is gone.

Jason thinks, *I'll never see you again. You created this mess. You are a bad person, and you will die a hungry, lonely man with plenty of time to wish you had done better. Goodbye and good riddance.*

Jason's inner monster is thrilled. This won't be a violent, quick death, but still satisfying.

Peter Owens has twenty-two days to live.

After day ten, he runs out of food. No boat returns with supplies. He has no phone reception to call and find out where his supplies are or contact Jason. On day fifteen, the solar power unit fails, and he cannot boil his drinking water. On day twenty-two, he dies of dehydration and starvation. Jason flies his small jet over the island and sees a body on the sand, and his inner demon is thrilled.

Giana soon forgets all about him. She's too busy with a B-list celebrity now, working her way up the alphabet of fame. She never thinks to ask after Peter.

Peter will never be found.

The family is delighted by Peter Owen's demise.

CHAPTER 15

THE GIFTED FAMILY MEMBERS SIT TOGETHER in Frank's office. Frank James, Sabrina, Kari, Jason, Nelson, and Lyndsey.

Frank is a shadow of his former self. He is sitting in his soft leather chair that seems to envelop him, watching the waves out of the window. He is there but not really. He is far off in his thoughts of a life well lived. He reminisces about all the adventures he had with his dad, George Francis, and all the lives they took. Lives that needed to be taken to make the world better. He and his inner monster are enjoying the past, unaware that the family is talking about important subjects.

Sabrina is now fully in charge of the gifted family members. Kari is a successful attorney who, with her law practice, has access to many red people and is an important source of information when required. Jason is still a pilot with successful killings under his belt. Nelson, his son, is growing up. Twenty years old, six feet tall, handsome with jet black hair, and well-built from all the time he spends at the college gym. He is taking after his dad as a private jet pilot. He is good-natured and fun to be with, but when family matters come up, he is all business. He has been introduced to his gift and knows that being careless can spell disaster for the family. He is learning the family business and promises to be an important future asset to the family.

Lyndsey has become an active member of the killing machine the family has created. Her career as a paramedic gives her skills that are useful to the family, and she has been able to bring about the demise of a few red people who are being transported by ambulance to the hospital. They weren't in real danger of death until they got into her ambulance.

Sabrina says to all, "The gift is always evolving. It is important that we never take it for granted and we protect each other. We must be able to fulfill our destiny and be able to murder the unworthy and not get caught."

Sabrina looks around the room at the five who have the family gift. Kari's family: her husband, Jason, and son, Nelson, who is growing up fast. And now Lyndsey, her daughter. Frank, too, is there but no longer counts, as he is a definite liability to the family. Sabrina will need to address this problem soon.

Jason speaks up. "I have eliminated two red people, Jackson Garwood and Peter Owens, and that has brought me pleasure, but my inner demon is calling for more. I have been keeping my eye on someone new. Her name is Sissy Andrews. She's a flight attendant for my company. She has been servicing our wealthy and celebrity clients on flights. She gets friendly with them and gains their confidence. Then she gets their money. Two of our wealthy clients have died recently under suspicious circumstances, and I've noticed that she's getting redder."

Jason looks at Kari and continues, "I will be piloting a jet trip for an A-list celebrity, Johnny Murphy, who has scheduled a trip for a few days with his friends. I thought this would be a good time to eliminate Sissy Andrews."

The heads around the room nod in approval. They now know that a death on an island a long way away is comforting. Easier to get away with.

Lyndsey says, "I am new to this, but my inner dark passenger requires me to get involved. I am not ready yet, but with your help, especially my mom," she nods to Sabrina, "I will be ready soon."

Sabrina looks at Kari, and they both nod to each other in a sad shaking of their heads. They both know the target for Lyndsey. Respect the target. Love the target. The future target is someone special. The time is coming. And soon. They all know.

Sabrina says, "Lyndsey, we have someone for you in the near future. We promise."

Lyndsey says, "Let me know. I am ready, but I think I know who you are considering, and I am sad. Ready but sad."

The family is evolving. As the family expands with new marriages and new births, Sabrina and Kari must keep watch over them, looking for the telltale sign of wispy red family members. As Lyndsey has shown, the inner monster can stay quiet and hibernate for a long period of time before showing itself. A keen eye on the family is required.

†

CHAPTER 16

JASON DEMPSEY IS IN HIS GULFSTREAM G280 JET, flying Johnny Murphy and seven of his friends to a rest and relaxation vacation in the Cayman Islands. The jet comes to a safe stop. The passengers depart and are driven to the fabulous Ritz-Carlton Hotel, steps from the famous seven-mile beach on Grand Cayman.

They have been drinking, laughing, and enjoying each other on the jet trip over. This week is planned to be a fun and relaxing time for all. Johnny Murphy says to Jason, "I've just wrapped up my third movie in the Darkside trilogy for the Marvel franchise, and this trip is a much-needed time for rest and fun before my next movie role starts. I'm slated to play the lead in the much-anticipated film, *Fear in the Irish Countryside*."

Jason says, "Enjoy yourself, and I'll be around when you are ready to depart."

Jason is there for a very different reason. To kill a red person up close and personal. He is excited, nervous, anticipatory, and scared, all at once. His dark passenger is thirsty for a kill.

He has set his eyes on Sissy Andrews. She wouldn't target Johnny because he's too young and savvy; she prefers older clients to cozy up to. Jason knows that during her stay on the Cayman Islands, she'll be out looking for ways to help herself to other people's wealth. Jason plans on bumping into her on this trip and eliminating her slowly.

He has brought along a small vial of the brown liquid that he will shoot into her neck to make her body useless but will keep her eyes and mind alert and her body able to feel but not able to move. A very handy brown liquid that goes back a few generations to George Francis, the family patriarch.

Johnny Murphy and his entourage are staying at the Ritz-Carlton. The Ritz-Carlton is used to A-list celebrities and will protect Johnny Murphy's privacy as best they can.

Jason is checked into a small, less-known hotel, Club Suites at Rum Point, a quiet but beautiful part of the island. Here he plans to bump into Sissy, who knows Jason as a pilot for the Jet Service they both work for.

Sissy is on the lookout for wealthy single men, but being single or married does not matter to Sissy. She is mainly looking at the wallet size. The more money they have, the more money for Sissy to steal. She is getting rich with her scheming ways. She will be all over the island looking for her target. Sissy thinks, *There are lots of loaded men here that would be* happy *to buy me dinner. Dinner and a treat. I need to find one or two on this trip to enrich me.*

She says out loud to herself, "I heard about the celebrity A-lister movie star, Johnny Murphy, being seen at the Ritz-Carlton on Seven Mile Beach. Maybe I'll go over to the Ritz-Carlton and see if I can bump into the famous Johnny Murphy. To marry a super-rich movie star would even be better than stealing from the fat old rich guys. I'm a little old for him, but if I can get the chance to be alone with him, I think I can prove to him I'm worth the age difference."

Jason follows her discreetly and watches her go into the Ritz-Carlton. He knows what she is up to. Johnny has security, and to bump into him is almost impossible. Jason knows this, so he goes into the hotel and walks up to the area Johnny is in. "Hey, Johnny. Are you getting the relaxation you were hoping for?"

"Jason! Come on in here and have a drink with us," says Johnny.

Jason joins Johnny and sits in a chaise lounge, enjoying the conversation and the spectacular aqua-blue Caribbean waters. He looks around for Sissy.

And there she is outside the celebrity area, looking in. She spots Jason and yells, "Hey, Jason, what are you doing here? Work? Come here for a second."

Jason gets up and goes to the ring of people trying to get a glimpse of Johnny. "Hi, Sissy, what are you doing here in the Cayman Islands? A job or relaxing?"

Sissy says, "Just some time off to relax. I would really love to meet Johnny Murphy. Any chance you can introduce me to him?"

Jason sees the redness glowing around her. He says, "Sure, no problem. He is only going to be here for a little while, then he's got plans, so it will have to be a quick hello and goodbye."

With that, Sissy is let inside the sacred circle to meet Johnny. Jason says, "Johnny, this is a colleague of mine. Sissy, this is Johnny Murphy, the one and only."

Johnny gets up and shakes hands with Sissy and says, "Sissy, nice to meet you. Are you enjoying your time in this wonderful place?"

Sissy says in her sexiest voice, "I am. I love all your movies. It is a pleasure to meet you. Perhaps we can spend some time together."

But Johnny is distracted and looks at his entourage and says, "Let's go, guys. The snorkeling is supposed to be spectacular at night. The boat awaits."

Sissy is disappointed she was not asked to go, but a proper introduction is just the first step. She will be ready the next time she gets the opportunity.

Jason pulls Sissy aside and whispers in her ear, "I happen to know that Johnny is going to have an intimate beach party tonight at Rum Point on the other side of the island. I can get you in. Meet me outside the Rum Point Club at midnight."

Sissy is excited and says, "I will be there, Jason. See you at midnight. Thanks!"

She thinks, *I'll be my best self tonight. He won't be able to resist me, especially in my little red bikini.*

Later that night, Jason is ready with two items in the pocket of his short-sleeved shirt. Two items he will use later. Sissy shows up right at midnight in a very revealing red bikini; a sheer blue chiffon robe over the top does not cover anything. Even Jason cannot look away.

"Want a quick dip while we wait for Johnny to get here? It should be in about fifteen minutes," says Jason.

"Sure," she says.

They shed their cover-ups and walk into the shallows. The waves lap over their ankles, knees, then waists as they wade in.

Sissy has fifteen minutes to live.

They both walk into the warm Caribbean water up to their shoulders and stare up at the moonlit night. Even now, Jason sees her glowing red. Jason has brought his two items with him. Jason is on edge for what is about to happen, and his mouth suddenly goes dry. He is here to do a job. They walk slowly and talk about the Cayman Islands, the delicious lobster available at every restaurant, and the tropical cocktails. When Sissy turns from him to admire the view of the beach, Jason thinks, *Now is the time.*

Jason quickly pushes the needle with the brown liquid into Sissy's neck. She is rendered instantly helpless. Her eyes are alert; her body is just dead weight. Jason holds her up, but her eyes plead. Jason says, "Sissy Andrews, I know what you have been doing, I know the clients you have been stealing from, and I suspect there are two wealthy clients you have killed for their money. Johnny will not be showing up here tonight. He never was. I am going to kill you here and now for all the damage you have caused. All because of money. Such a shame, but you have earned this; you deserve this."

Sissy is terrified. She thinks, *How did I get here? How did I get caught? Help me. Save me.* She realizes that there is no way out. Death is staring at her. She can feel the warm water on her skin and knows Jason is holding her up. *Is he going to drown me?*

Jason is behind her with the back of her head on his chest. She is floating helplessly in the warm water. He can sense her thoughts. "No, Sissy, I am not going to drown you," he says.

Jason then pulls out a knife and cuts each of her wrists. Her eyes are screaming, her breathing accelerated, her body betraying her. Jason makes a second cut to both wrists. The warm waters are carrying her life's blood away. Diluted in the Caribbean Sea.

Her eyes begin to fade, her breathing begins to slow, and she begins to give up on life. She has no choice. Jason says, "Sissy, this is the ending you get for killing old rich men for their fortunes. To trick them, to get them involved with your schemes. There is a penalty, and this is it."

Her breathing begins to be shallow; her soul is about to leave her and go where?

Jason does not know. But Sissy Andrews is about to find out whatever is beyond this life.

Sissy knows she is almost gone. *This is what I get for stealing money? This is so not worth it,* she thinks to herself.

Then Sissy is gone.

Jason is electric; his inner demon is excited. Jason is pleased that this one up-close and personal death is going so well. Jason has gotten away with his one murder. But what's that sound?

"Hey, who's out there?" comes a shout from a boat drifting by.

Jason can see an old, crusty boater with a white beard. He is shining a light in Jason's direction, and he panics. He lets Sissy's body go, and she sinks below the surface, and he holds her body down.

He calms his breathing and gives the guy a wave. "Just taking a night swim, sir! Nothing to be worried about. I'm a strong swimmer!"

"I wouldn't swim out this far. There have been shark sightings these past few nights," says the man.

Jason's heart leaps. All this blood in the water could attract several sharks.

"Right. Thanks for the information. I'll swim back now. I appreciate you checking on me," he says. "You can get along now."

The old man nods and turns his little motorboat around. But Jason is too concerned about sharks to feel relief. He swims as fast as he can back to shore, imagining a great white behind him.

Jason gets to shore, picks up his and Sissy's cover-ups, and walks away. He puts her red cover-up in a restaurant's trash container, mixed in with all the wet food garbage, and it disappears from sight. Jason's dark passenger is pleased. Jason is aglow.

He reports back to the others with the family gift. All the inner monsters are pleased. The thirst has been quenched. For now.

Sissy is never found, and Jason wonders if the currents took her away or the hungry sharks had a meal.

CHAPTER 17

THROUGH THE YEARS, the family has stayed strong and unified. The kill team works as a unit, and its members help and protect each other. Jason has had the last kill. Sissy Andrews was never found in the shark-infested waters of the Cayman Islands.

The family has successfully been eliminating red people, but Frank James is now a liability to the family. He talks to himself constantly, under his breath but loud enough for people to hear if they listen to his mumbling. He is reminiscing about his father, George Francis, and the killings they did together, and the killings Frank did alone. They are constantly on his mind and his tongue. He understands little of what is going on and lives in his mind. Occasionally he is lucid, but not often anymore. It is time to do something.

Sabrina has a talk with Kari, and, sadly, they both agree that Frank will be the undoing of the family if the wrong person finds out about the family gift. Frank needs to be eliminated. The person they think should eliminate Frank is Lyndsey, who is ready to assume her place in the family club.

Kari sits with Lyndsey. "Lyndsey, it is time for your Uncle Frank to leave us. He could potentially expose our family if he were to be around someone that was interested in what he is saying. Do you think you can eliminate him? His time has come."

Lyndsey gulps hard. "I thought my first kill would be Uncle Frank. I hate to do it, but I am honored to be the family member to be with him through the end."

Sabrina nods. "I was the one to bring my beloved father's days to an end. He was happy for me to do it, as my brother will be when you release him from this world."

Kari says, "It is a sad necessity that our family eliminate an older family member rather than take the chance we could all be exposed. We will all be with you at our next family meeting on Wednesday. I will bring a vial of the brown liquid."

Wednesday comes quickly for Lyndsey, but she is ready and has the right mindset, and her inner monster is hungry. She has to steady herself. Right herself. She knows she will do this, but she is uneasy and tense. It's important to see it through; once she starts, she must not stop because it would be unfair to her uncle.

Sabrina, Kari, Jason, Nelson, Lyndsey, and Frank are together in Frank's office, as they have been so many times before. Sabrina is uneasy but tells Frank, "Come here, brother, and sit on the sofa between me and Lyndsey."

Frank nods and shuffles over and sits down on the sofa. Frank is lucid for a moment, then he is mumbling. Lyndsey looks over at Sabrina, takes a deep breath, then pulls out the brown liquid vial and sticks it into Frank's neck. He turns, surprised, feeling the sting of the needle, but quickly he slumps against the sofa back. She continues to be tense and apprehensive because this is her uncle. A dear person to her.

His eyes brighten and enlarge. He knows what is happening. He had been there when Sabrina did the same thing to their father. He is not frightened but elated. He looks around the room with his eyes still fully alert. He sees his family around him, all in red, and he is pleased. They are all here for him at the end. His inner monster is confused but excited that a kill is about to take place. Frank thinks, *I am ready. I have lived a full life. A different life from almost anyone on earth, but a satisfying life. My end is here and now. I'm glad it is Lyndsey.* Then his thoughts are gone, and Frank is incoherent again.

Frank's body feels like it is made out of stone. No movement is possible, but he feels Sabrina holding his hand. Her hand is warm, a comforting connection. Lyndsey looks at her uncle Frank. Frank blinks at Lyndsey, letting her know, *It's okay. Do what you have to do; I'm ready.*

Lyndsey looks deep into the eyes of her beloved uncle before she puts her strong hands around his neck and applies pressure. Lyndsey is nervous and sad but resolved to finish what she has started. Frank is emotional. He is feeling what death is like. His breathing does not accelerate like most victims because he knows what to expect. He is amazed at how it all feels.

Tightened pressure on his neck gives him a new sensation: panic. Frank looks at Lyndsey, then at Sabrina. For the briefest of moments he has fear in his eyes, but it quickly passes. Sabrina rubs his cool hand, and Lyndsey applies more pressure. He has done this to so many, and for a brief moment he panics, but then he relaxes into this death dance with both Sabrina and Lyndsey.

Frank's eyes begin to close; his last breath is near. Lyndsey and Frank are connecting forever; both are experiencing raw emotions. The next world is fast approaching. His inner monster is delighted, confused, electric, and sad all at once. Once more, Lyndsey squeezes, and a tear escapes from her eye, but her inner monster, her dark passenger, is beyond excited.

Then Frank James is no more.

After a long moment, each member of the family with the gift respectfully places their hands on his head and shoulder as a sign of love and respect for this man who has guided the family for so long.

Kari says, "May his journey be one of discovery and amazement."

Uncle Frank is gone. Lyndsey has committed an up-close and personal murder. She is invigorated but also sad to see her Uncle Frank eliminated.

But the family gift is preserved.

All is good.

CHAPTER 18

FRANK JAMES IS DEAD. His death is ruled as natural causes because the family has mastered their gift so well. A true skill. He is laid to rest next to his beloved wife, Carla. Frank's funeral is spectacular, with attendance by the entire police department. His old friend Michael Jacobson is there to pay his respects. His family and friends all speak well of Frank and his extraordinary life. The day is one of a life well lived, a day to celebrate Frank and all he stood for. Stories are told, good times remembered, and love shared throughout the crowd. Frank James will be missed. The public does not know the whole story. Nobody ever will.

The funeral is a success, and Frank James is laid to rest. A new family chapter is beginning.

Someone is paying attention to all that is happening and all that has been happening.

Tiffany Rose, Lyndsey's sister, is becoming more and more curious about the family. Her family. She is noticing that certain family members seem to be gathering together often, and she is not included. There is a secret that binds them, and she wants to know what it is.

Her once timid big sister now has a confidence that cannot be described. An air of conviction after her ordeal with the kidnapper. Lyndsey came out of that experience a different person. Tiffany got all the details talking with Lyndsey, but there was something she was not telling her. Something important. Tiffany Rose can feel the air thick with secrets. She watches at family functions and keeps an eye on Uncle Frank's office and discovers there is an undercurrent in the family. Something is happening, and she wants in.

One day, Tiffany confronts Lyndsey, who denies any secret family society. Tiffany Rose talks to her dad, Sam, but Sam says, "I know nothing about any secret family meetings."

Finally, Tiffany Rose goes to her mom and says, "I can see with my own two eyes that there is an inner circle within the family. I can see you all conspiring, but I don't know what is going on. Please tell me or include me."

Sabrina looks at Tiffany Rose, her youngest daughter, and says, "Tiffany Rose, we are a close family, and we all have our little secrets and jokes. I think you are misunderstanding what you see."

"No, Mom. Don't patronize me. I want to know what's going on."

But Sabrina sticks to her guns. She thinks, *If you are not with the family gift, if you don't see red, then you cannot know. You are not included.*

"Tiffany, there is nothing that you need to be concerned about," says Sabrina.

But Tiffany Rose is not about to let go of this.

She watches.

The family decides that Sabrina and her family will move into Frank's house and reside there. Sabrina, Sam, Lyndsey, and Tiffany Rose. The office where certain family members meet is now Sabrina's. The ocean views are still breathtaking; the colorful art is replaced with even more colorful art that Sabrina loves, and, in the corner, where Frank kept his detective trophies and mementos, Sabrina's novels are now displayed. Her collection is now up to nine. She is successful enough with her books, and they produce an income she is proud of. There are more books to come. She does, after all, have a good source of stories. Her latest novel, *Murder in the Caribbean*, is front and center with all her books displayed.

The gifted family members are seated. It is strange that Frank James is not present, but the family needs to continue on and evolve. An empty chair is there to honor Frank. Each family member at the meeting, before they sit down, respectfully touches the chair as a tribute to him.

Just as they are starting to talk, the door bursts open. Tiffany Rose strides into the middle of the room and proclaims, "I am not sure what this meeting is about, but I don't want any more secrets." She pauses. "Uncle Jason? Nelson? You're here too? Whatever this is, I want to be included."

The family sits dumbfounded, keenly aware that someone has crashed their inner circle. Not just anyone, but a family member who seems to not have a bit of red in her. Not even the smallest glow.

She definitely does not have the family gift.

Sabrina looks around the room. Every face is looking back at her. What do they do? Sabrina is Tiffany Rose's mother, but she is also the leader of this family and cannot let anyone without the family gift have admittance. Or could she?

How did Tiffany learn about the meetings? How has she been so observant that she has perpetrated the secrecy of the family?

Sabrina starts by saying, "Tiffany, tell us how you were able to find out about our meeting and our quiet discussions, and what did we do to tip you off that something was happening?"

Tiffany says, "I noticed some family members talking and then shutting up when someone not in your group tried to participate in a conversation. You've not exactly been discreet. Again, I don't know what is going on here, but I want to be a part of it. If only to show you all that what you are doing is being noticed. I can be your 'heads-up' when things seem off or someone is beginning to suspect something."

Sabrina is the head of this group, and as head, she has every right to lead, to make adjustments, and to travel the right path for future generations. She puts her pointer finger and thumb along her chin with her head down and thinks for a few minutes. The room is silent, waiting. When she looks up, she says, "Tiffany, the family members you see before you in this room have a gift that we did not ask for, a gift we cannot dispose of; it is a burden and an honor."

She explains the gift as carefully as she can, adding, "The gift gives us the ability to kill without remorse or guilt. We possess a dark passenger, an inner monster, a demon within us that craves death. The dark passenger is calculating, devious, determined, and somewhat patient, while the inner monster is emotional, terrifying, strong, unrelenting, and aggressive. They are different, and some of us have one or the other. Some of us have both. We do not get to choose. It is chosen for us at birth. Our inner monsters demand we eliminate certain people who show up with a red aura. But, Tiffany, with you, we see no red, not even a wispy red. You do not have, nor can you obtain, the inner dark passenger. Lyndsey found the inner monster when she was put under tremendous stress by a kidnapper. Her inner monster took over, and Lyndsey had superhuman strength when it was required of her to protect herself. We were shocked, and we do not expect that to happen again to anyone—"

Tiffany interrupts, "So, if it happened to Lyndsey, maybe it would happen to me if I were in danger?"

"Perhaps, but we cannot simply stage a dangerous situation to find out," Kari says, smiling kindly at her.

"Are you not upset by all this, Tiffany?" Sabrina asks. "You don't think we are crazy or evil?"

Tiffany shakes her head. "No. I don't know why, but I understand in here," she says, touching her chest. "Like, it makes complete sense. Maybe that means I do have the gift, sort of, just not in the way that you all have."

Sabrina nods and looks thoughtful. "I'm happy to hear you say that. We need to protect the family, and we have trusted you with this enormous secret. You must promise to always keep this secret, even from the people closest to you, throughout your life."

"I promise," says Tiffany solemnly.

"Although you cannot be one of us, since you do not have the inner demon that requires you to kill, you have an inquisitive nature, and you can teach us things we can no longer feel or see. You can monitor us so that we do not arouse more suspicion or give away any of our secrets through our actions. We can and will allow you in this circle, but not to kill. You will not put yourself in jeopardy. If any one of us gets caught, we all get caught. We must retain our secret nature. We will accept you, but all in this office must place their hand on your shoulders as a sign of support for my proposition. You must not mention this to any other human outside this room. If other family members receive this gift, we will all welcome them."

With that, each member of the family steps up and places a gentle hand on Tiffany's shoulders in a sign of support and keeps their hand there until Sabrina gives her approval.

The family is expanding in new ways. The family is evolving.

†

CHAPTER 19

SABRINA IS CONCERNED THAT TIFFANY ROSE has been admitted to a club that only usually lets in family members with the family gift. Everyone is concerned about how Tiffany will fit in to help the family. The only person not concerned is Tiffany.

Tiffany has a secret that she discovered about herself long ago, which she has not yet shared because she isn't sure how to explain it. But hearing her mother explain the gift, she is certain she has a special form of it. Rather than seeing a redness in people, there are some people who appear to Tiffany as near-invisible. They are an outline of a person. She researched neurological and even psychiatric conditions but was unable to discover what might be going on. Knowing her family's secret makes her feel less crazy, but she is still concerned about what it means. There are very few of these transparent people, but she sees perhaps one or two a week. She thinks, *It's time to let my family know. Perhaps they can help me with this mystery.*

Little does she know she will be unleashing the inner demons, the dark passenger, and the inner monsters in a new direction.

At the next family meeting, Tiffany says to the gathering, "I love that you have the faith in me to allow me at your meetings. You all know I do not see red people as you do, but since I was very young, I have seen people who walk among us that are . . . I guess 'colorless' is the only way I can describe it. I mean, I can see their outline, as if they have been sketched by a pencil. I need help deciphering what I am seeing. I think it must be important."

Everyone has been listening intently, and they all look at each other confused. But they aren't shocked. The gift has been changing in ways they've never seen before. Why would this be any different?

Lyndsey speaks up: "Tiffany, let me work with you to try and understand what you are seeing."

Nelson speaks next: "Me too."

Sabrina is happy that Nelson has something to do that doesn't involve the killings. He's too young and she wants to protect him as long as possible. She says, "Excellent. You all work together during the next few weeks and report back to us what you find out about how this curious phenomenon works. It certainly is interesting. Now, is there anything new on people we have been watching?"

Jason talks about an interesting passenger that he has had contact with because of the great amount of flying this person has been doing lately. His name is Juan Pablo, and he has a habit of having girlfriends disappear, die, or have mental breakdowns. Juan is a Wall Street financial consultant heading his own small but extremely successful hedge fund called Alamo Square.

He is neon red.

Jason adds, "I am taking him to Flores Island, in the Azores, Portuguese islands in the Atlantic, next Tuesday for a five-day retreat with his girlfriend, Taylor, and two clients. Come with us then. We will both get a better picture of who this Juan Pablo really is."

"Great," says Sabrina. "I'll be there."

On Tuesday, bright and early, the Gulfstream G280 jet with Jason as pilot and Sabrina as flight attendant takes off for Flores Island with four passengers.

Juan Pablo is an easy passenger. "Sabrina, can we have some breakfast?" he asks. And later, "Can we have some drinks for everyone?" Juan Pablo seems to care for Taylor and has a relaxed nature with his two clients. They are to stay in a residence high above the Atlantic Ocean with breathtaking views with a chef and two servants to take care of their every need. As the passengers disembark, Jason says, "Enjoy your time here. We will see you on Tuesday."

When they all reappear after five days, the men all look happy and talkative, but Taylor is quiet and keeps her eyes down. Something is up, and Sabrina is determined to find out what.

After the passengers are fed and are taking naps across the wide Atlantic, Sabrina pulls Taylor aside in the back room and asks, "Taylor, what happened? You were so full of life when the trip started, but now you look beat down and defeated."

Taylor peeks around Sabrina to see if anyone can listen, then nervously says, "Juan Pablo seems to be a nice guy, but I saw another side of him on this trip. He is demanding, forceful, and demeaning. He treated me badly and let his clients too. There was nothing I could do. I am so ashamed."

Sabrina says, "Taylor, this was not your fault. Look, I have the means and the way to deal with Juan Pablo and his two clients, but I need your help."

Taylor nods.

Sabrina says, "We will stop at Bermuda, telling him that we need to check something with the plane. While you're there, suggest a short trip. No need to even check into a hotel. Just to stop, swim, snorkel, and then back on the jet and get back home. A small side diversion."

Taylor says, "I can do that, but what are you thinking?"

Sabrina says, "Maybe a little payback. Leave it with me."

She's thinking about somewhere Jason has talked about, a cave that floods twice a day with the tides. Something exciting but dangerous.

Taylor goes to a sleeping Juan Pablo, gently wakes him, and whispers into his ear.

Soon Jason is making a small detour to Bermuda for the afternoon. Sabrina makes the reservations for a cave adventure, and the jet is met by an ancient-looking man, Diego, who looks as old as the stone that covers the island. Sabrina joins them, and they drive off from the small airport to a boat dock. Everyone gets in the boat, and out to the aquamarine waters of the Bermuda Islands they go. The old man drives the slow, old boat to a private island, where he suggests a cave on the far side of the small island that is begging to be explored and snorkeled in. They all agree, and the boat steers into the cave entrance.

There are crystals hanging from the ceiling of the cave, and the waters are a magnificent blue. And the cave only gets better the deeper they go. After a while, the boat can go no further. They get out and proceed on foot down the spectacular cave, but without the men realizing it, Sabrina takes Taylor back toward the boat. Taylor looks confused, but Sabrina reassures her.

Juan Pablo is completely engrossed in the cave and encourages his two clients to go further and further into the cave. The old man warns him, "Gentlemen, it's best not to go any deeper into this cave. The tides will be coming back before long, and there is a chance bad things could happen if we don't start back now. The tides here can come in quicker than you might guess. Then we would be stuck here at least for the night. Not a good thing. The deeper you go, the more chances you take."

"No way," says Juan Pablo, "this cave is just too amazing. I want to see more. *We* want to see more."

The old man says, "You three are on your own. I'm going back before the tides roar in. The girls are back at the boat already. This is not safe." He makes a convincing protest, but Sabrina has paid him extra not to insist the men return with him as he would normally do. He was disgusted by what he'd heard about what Taylor had endured and was only too happy to take Sabrina's instructions. He gives the men some headlamps and leaves them to their fate.

Juan says, "Go on, old man; we will be fine. We won't be long, I promise, but we can't go now; we've never seen anything like this." Juan Pablo and his clients continue down the path deeper into the cave.

Juan Pablo and his clients have four hours to live.

After only half an hour alone, they realize the water is rising. "Come on, man, let's go," says one of the clients. Juan Pablo agrees, but their way out is already filled with water. They find a ledge in the rock to sit on, believing that either they'll be rescued or that the water will recede again in a few hours and they can escape.

But the water keeps rising, up to their ledge, and they spend four cold, wet, miserable hours being tossed about in the dark cave. Juan is petrified and shaken; his clients are panic-stricken and terrified, trapped in the beautiful but deadly cave with no way out. The ocean is rushing in at an unbelievable pace. The water is warm, but that brings little comfort to the trapped men. The space for air is getting smaller and smaller. They tread water trying to get a bit of breath at the cave's ceiling. They are exhausted with the effort. They all feel the heavy hand of death on them. And soon they look forward to death to put them out of this hell on earth.

Meanwhile, the old man takes Sabrina and Taylor back to the main island. "Those men made their decision. Their deaths are their choice," he mumbles, mad that they thought they knew better than him, who has lived his entire life in these caves, caverns, and pockets of glory that mark the islands. Too many caves to count. But he is also pleased that these terrible men have got what they deserve.

Sabrina nods to Diego, then winks at Taylor and says, “Time to get you back on the jet and get you home.”

Before they depart, they contact the police and tell the story of three men going deep into a cave and never returning. A story the police hear often. The police make a report but put no effort into a rescue mission. The men are fish food by now.

Juan Pablo and his clients are never heard from again. Juan Pablo is no more.

CHAPTER 20

TIFFANY ROSE, HER SISTER, LYNDSEY, AND COUSIN, NELSON, sit looking at each other with the question, who are these semitransparent people that only Tiffany can see? What do these people mean? The family is interested. Tiffany describes them as ghostlike. She can see an image, but the person is hard to define. But what are these images? Tiffany, Lyndsey, and Nelson are about to find out. The three of them have been looking for two days without luck. These people are not everywhere and are more difficult to find. Lyndsey wonders if her sister is being honest with them or lying to get in on the family business.

Then, Tiffany is studying people walking by as she eats lunch with Lyndsey and Nelson at the Brass Cup. Suddenly, she perks up. "There is one now, with a pink shirt on. He looks ghostly to me." Both Lyndsey and Nelson quickly look at a young man walking by with a pink shirt, jeans, and Johnston & Murphy tennis shoes. He looks like a regular guy to them. Lyndsey is still skeptical. Nevertheless, she throws down money on the table for the meal, and they all leave the restaurant to follow this young man.

He is walking slowly, looking at this window display and that window display. He's in no real hurry. He checks his watch, then picks up the pace and walks into High Park Hair Salon. Lyndsey says, "When he comes out, I will bump into him and see if I can strike up a conversation with him and simply ask him his name."

Nelson says, "The old-fashioned way, huh?"

Lyndsey laughs. The young man stays in the hair salon for about an hour, and then as he is leaving, Lyndsey walks beside him and simply says, "That's a pretty good haircut you have there."

The young man smiles and says, "Why, thank you."

"I'm Lyndsey," she says.

"Hey. I'm Oliver. Your hair looks pretty good too," he says.

He gives her sideways looks as they walk together along the street. Who is she? Is she trying to pick him up or just being friendly? They walk and talk until they come to the Hampton Arms, an upscale residential development.

"Well, this is where I live," he says to Lyndsey. "Thanks for your company."

He nods at the doorman, who opens the lobby door and says, "Good afternoon, Mr. Bronson."

"Good afternoon, Higgins," Oliver says. He looks at Lyndsey, then says, "It's been nice meeting you, Lyndsey. I hope to see you around." And walks into the lobby.

Lyndsey smiles because this man did not hit on her as she expected he might. He was a complete gentleman. Nelson comes up to her and says, "Well, that seemed to work out. Did you get his name?"

"I did, Oliver Bronson," says Lyndsey.

Now they have a name, and they can find out more about him and why he might be ghostly to Tiffany.

They go to Lyndsey's place and spread out their laptops and begin researching the life of Oliver Bronson. Records indicate that he seems to be a typical thirty-year-old, college-educated, moderately successful attorney. No girlfriend but a few close friends. He seems innocent enough, but he is a loner in a lot of ways. Is this a hint?

Then Nelson hits a nugget. "Hey, this guy is a relative of Ralph Walsh, the serial killer who was caught and executed over twenty years ago."

They all stop and look at each other. What does this mean? Is he a potential threat? Does he carry violent genes?

Nelson says, "Well, it could be a clue. But we need you to point out another semitransparent person to us, Tiff. If another person is also related to a killer, then we may be on to something."

Tiffany says, "I only run into these images occasionally. It might take a while to spot another one. I will try to get their names, like Lyndsey did."

Two days later, Tiffany calls Lyndsey. She says, "I spotted another one and watched him get baseball tickets for the Triple-A minor league baseball team for a Saturday game. I stood behind him at the box office and picked up three tickets for that game for the three of us."

That Saturday, they are seated in the stadium watching an exciting game, a score of six to eight in only the third inning. A lot of baseball action. The crowd is cheering and having a fun time. Seated below them in the same section is the man Tiffany has identified. He sits with two girls. To Tiffany, his ghostly lack of color stands out because the fans are all dressed in red and yellow to support the team. Like all minor league games, the stands are about half full with fans. There is a lot of room to move around.

Tiffany says, "I have an idea," and she moves from her seat to a seat just above this semitransparent man and says in a loud voice, "Oh my god! Barry, is that you?"

She puts her hand on the guy's shoulder, but the guy reacts angrily and says, "Get the hell away from me."

Tiffany says in a quiet voice, "I am so, so sorry. You looked like a cousin of mine that I had not seen in forever. I apologize. My name is

Jane Southers," and she puts out her hand to shake.

"Yeah, no problem, I'm Bernhard Bauer. Sorry to bark at you," he replies, and he shakes her hand.

Tiffany goes back to her seat and nods at Lyndsey and Nelson. "I got his name."

Lyndsey says, "The two girls with him are not red nor transparent. Let's go and do some research."

They return to Lyndsey's place and begin to research Bernhard Bauer. It takes them little time to find out that Bauer is a German name and that he is a descendant of one of that country's most known serial killers, Von Riech, who was put to death many years ago. This discovery is the confirmation that these people are linked to evil people and perhaps have inherited their evil traits. The inner monsters are interested.

But Tiffany Rose, Lyndsey, and Nelson decide they need one more connection to prove this theory beyond doubt. Lyndsey no longer thinks her sister is lying for attention, but they need solid information before they can go to the family to discuss their findings. The family will be interested; the inner demons will be *very* interested. Tiffany is the only family member with the ability to see these people. So, she goes back to work waiting, searching for another semitransparent person to cross her path.

Finally, there he is. A tall man in his midtwenties eating lunch at Terry's Outdoor Dining. He is hard for Tiffany to see because he is more than the regular degree of transparency, but he is there.

She quickly calls Lyndsey and Nelson. "I'm on Main Street at Terry's Outdoor Dining, and there is another person of interest. He is different from the others in that I'm having a hard time seeing him at all; he is almost invisible to me. Please hurry over."

Within ten minutes they are all seated, looking at this man two tables over. Lyndsey gasps when she first sees him. He is also neon red.

Tiffany does not have the family gift to see the red color, but Tiffany's gift might be just as useful.

"We have got to find out about this guy. He is red, meaning he has done some harm against humanity either physically or mentally recently. His transparency also tells us he has a family history of cruelty," says Lyndsey.

They watch him, but he pays with cash, not a credit card. No paper trail. He leaves the restaurant and walks through town and through the park, looking right and left. He is looking for something. But what? They keep him in sight and make sure they are not spotted.

Then, he walks over to a park bench. An attractive young woman is at the other end. He does not look at her or talk to her. He ignores her, and she does the same to him. Both seem engrossed in their respective phones. She eventually gets up and heads away. He gets up a few moments afterward, following her from a distance. After a ten-minute walk, she goes into an apartment building, and he watches with interest as she goes in. He hangs around for a while, staring at the door, then walks away.

This gets the curiosity of the family trio, and the need to identify this suspicious person is now important. The girl in the apartment could be in jeopardy. They follow him carefully for about a mile when he goes into another apartment building. They watch him go into apartment 424. They go to the mailbox cluster and look at 424.

It says *R. Juarez.*

Lyndsey, Nelson, and Tiffany go back to Lyndsey's. They pull out their laptops and begin going to work, trying to discover who R. Juarez is. The team is hard at work. They find out R is for Riley, and then it does not take long to discover that this mysterious guy is a descendant of Richard Juarez, the so-called Hillside Killer, who terrorized a community forty years ago by showing up in the middle of the night to kill and maim. But why is he so red? What has he been doing, and what is he planning to do to the girl he secretly followed home from the park? That can't be good.

They have the information they need to go to the family council, but they are worried about the young lady and feel that they had better watch him and her for a few nights.

Nelson says to Lyndsey and Tiffany, "I think this guy is dangerous and that he has been prowling and killing in this area. He has moved two times in the last two years, and the places he has moved from have seen fewer murders after he leaves. This area is now dangerous for everyone with him here, especially at night. I say we watch him for the next few nights." Lyndsey and Tiffany agree. Nelson says, "I'll take the night shifts. You two can watch him during the days."

On the first night, Nelson watches Riley Juarez leave his apartment at three o'clock, dressed in dark clothing and walking toward the apartment of the young woman he followed from the park. Nelson quickly gets around him on the approach to the apartment building.

His heart hammering, he says, "Hey, how are you doing?"

Juarez stares at him, trying to place this man who seems to know who he is, but he can't. Juarez puts his hands in his pockets, turns around, and walks away.

Nelson tells Lyndsey and Tiffany of his encounter. "I think I stopped him from going into that girl's apartment. But I think he'll try again tonight; I just scared him off for the moment. I am going to wait for him tonight. I know I don't have approval from the family to have an up-close and personal kill, but I think tonight will be my night. My inner monster is thirsty, and I am ready." Nelson continues, "I need to do this on my own, but I do need a vial of Papa George's stuff to help me."

Lyndsey says, "I'll get you the brown liquid and bring it to you around five today."

Nelson is waiting at Riley Juarez's apartment with his precious vial. He is waiting; he is ready, but he is also tense. Riley is a tall man and looks strong. He is also used to conflict and confrontation. Nelson hopes his plan will work. He has a backup plan, as well as a backup plan to that backup plan. You can never be too ready. When circumstances change, you have to be able to adjust on the fly. This is a dangerous game they play. A serious game. A deadly game.

Around the same time as the night before, all dressed in black, Riley opens his front door, only to be met by Nelson, all dressed in black. "No, sir, go right back into your unit," he says as he pushes him back in the door. Riley may be surprised, but he is quickly on the offensive and fighting Nelson with all his might, which is considerable. Nelson is prepared but stunned that Riley is so strong and quick. The fight is on. They swing, hit each other, crash to the floor, and fight for their lives. Nelson hits Riley right above his right ear, which stops Riley for a moment as his ears ring. In this moment, Nelson inserts the needle into Riley's neck and sends the brown liquid coursing deep through his body. Riley goes limp. His eyes are bright and looking right and left, looking into Nelson's face. His body is immobile. Nelson struggles to get Riley's body to a leather chair. Nelson slumps at the base of that chair and takes a minute to shake the fight off. To reset his body. Then Nelson looks Riley square in the face to give him the little speech he has prepared.

"Riley, you have killed your last human. The girl in 113 is safe, and you will never bother her. My name is Nelson, and certain members of my family are dedicated to removing your kind from the face of the earth. We know you are related to the Hillside Killer, Richard Juarez. Perhaps you didn't know that yourself. But it's not your ancestor who's the problem now: you are. You are about to die by my hands. Whatever afterlife awaits, you are about to go there. I don't know where you will end up, but I hope it is not nice. You have earned whatever awaits you."

Riley Juarez is breathing at an accelerated speed, his eyes begging to talk, but he will never talk again. Nelson is ready and determined to carry out the next phase in this clash between good and evil. He puts his hands tightly around Riley's neck and applies pressure, entering the death dance. Riley is panicked; he is frightened; he is passing over. Nelson increases the pressure, being careful not to leave marks. The medical examiner may suspect strangulation, but a heart attack will be just as good a guess as to the cause of death. Nelson knows the brown liquid will have dissipated in Riley's system by the time he is found.

Nelson watches Riley's eyes start to cloud over; his body relaxes, and his soul leaves his body. Nelson continues to keep the pressure on. Nelson is thrilled; his inner monster is electric. His dark passenger is pleased; his demon is invigorated. His emotions are off the scale.

Riley Juarez is gone, and the monsters are pleased.

The dark fingers of death have collected another victim.

CHAPTER 21

THE FAMILY MEETS BACK IN SABRINA'S OFFICE. Sabrina, Kari, Jason, Lyndsey, Nelson, and Tiffany. Frank James is still missed by all, and his absence is noticeable. The empty chair honors his memory.

Lyndsey is there to explain what she, Nelson, and Tiffany have discovered about Tiffany's gift. Lyndsey says, "Tiffany pointed out three people. When we did our research, we discovered all of them were descendants of evil people. But only one of the three also showed up red. Neither Oliver Bronson, a relative of serial killer Ralph Walsh, nor Bernhard Bauer, a relative of German serial killer Von Riech, shows any deep red. What we are thinking is that these two have evil in their family past but are not actively dangerous themselves. People to watch, perhaps, but they are not at this time showing any deep red, so they are not people we would consider to kill. Our demons would not approve."

Nelson adds, "But the third man we followed was Riley Juarez, related to Richard Juarez, known as the Hillside Killer. Riley was neon red, and we watched as he was lining up his next victim. We felt we had to act quickly to protect an innocent girl that he was following. I grabbed him just as he was about to go out to kill this girl. The upshot is, I eliminated him."

The entire room is silent with shock at the news of Nelson's first up-close and personal kill, but there is static in the air. The telling of the killing has activated the inner monsters, the dark passengers. Everyone is excited and thrilled. Sabrina lets the celebration go on until everyone seems to settle back down.

Kari, who is surprised and pleased at the news, says, "Congratulations, son. Are you okay?"

Nelson grins. "I am totally fine. It was a strange experience, but it felt right. It was my destiny."

Kari gets up and goes over to her son, hugging him where he sits and kissing the top of his head. "That is good news. You've done well, Nelson," she says. "But I wish you'd have told me what you were going to do. We are all in this together, supporting each other. I don't like that you acted alone in this. Promise me you will always confide in the family before you take any such actions in the future."

Nelson nods. "Sure, Mom. Of course, I will keep everyone in the loop from now on. Do we have any other red people that are currently killing and need our family's attention?"

Everyone laughs. Nelson is all business.

Sabrina says, "Tiffany, we want you to stay on the lookout for semi-transparent people. And as Nelson says, do we have anyone for us to focus on?"

Lyndsey, back in her seat, says, "I have been watching a guy named Burton Douglas, who's a marine biologist who takes students out on day trips to show them marine life. There's a rumor that he separated one of the girls from the group and molested her before returning to the group. The girls don't talk to authorities for fear of being dropped from the class. This Burton Douglas has been getting away with this for too long. His red neon glow tells me he is ready to be dealt with. Nelson, I was hoping that you could help me. I have a plan, but I do need muscle and someone to help me out when I spring the trap."

Nelson is instantly alert and says, "I would love to help out my cousin anytime. I'm in."

Sabrina asks for a rough outline of what the plan is. The family listens with amazement to the plan and the fact that Lyndsey has come so far.

The inner monsters are thirsty, and this plan has woken them up. The room is abuzz for a second time today.

Sabrina approves and wishes Lyndsey and Nelson, "Good hunting."

Lyndsey has entered college, posing as a student in Burton's biology class. Soon, she is on the field trip with Burton Douglas. On this trip, she is on the RIB or rigid-hull inflatable boat that holds eighteen people, traveling along the ocean shoreline and looking for organisms and ecosystems.

Burton has been looking at Lyndsey the whole trip, and Lyndsey does not disappoint with her tight sweater and bashful looks back to Burton. Burton pulls the boat ashore in a small sand cove and has everyone get out to examine the environment.

He calls, "Jan and Lyndsey, you two please follow me up to the clifftop to look for other living ecosystems."

"Yes, sir," they both reply and fall in behind their teacher. What Burton does not know is that Lyndsey and Nelson were here the day before, looking for a special place to lure Burton. And they found it. Now it is just waiting for the right moment. As they travel up this slope, they see many interesting specimens to look at and talk about.

"Jan, would you stay in this area and note the interesting marine life while Lyndsey and I go further up the trail?"

"Sure," says Jan.

Lyndsey follows Burton a short distance, then says in a sexy voice, "I want to be the leader. Maybe I can find something that will interest you?"

Burton is all in. To watch Lyndsey from behind is a pleasure. Lyndsey, in her tight jeans and tighter sweater, goes off course and is on some treacherous rocks. He is excited to get his hands on Lyndsey. He wants to grab her, but she is too far ahead. "Hey, hold up, Lyndsey. I'm trying. You are too fast for me," says Burton with lust in his voice.

She goes faster and, at the right time, jumps behind a rock pile and says, "Come on, slowpoke, catch up." Lyndsey is concerned and worried that Burton will either jump over the rocks or the rocks will not release and trap him. The moment of truth is now.

He has not seen Lyndsey go around that pile of rocks, and when Burton steps there, the rock gives way. "What the hell?" he yells as he lets out a yelp. He quickly sinks up to his armpits. His lower body is trapped, and he is so tight in this space that it takes his breath away.

Lyndsey, excited to hear his pleas for help, turns around and walks back to Burton, trapped tightly in the rock grave. Nelson comes out from behind some rocks and goes to Burton. Rather than pull him up, he pushes hard down on him, assuring that he cannot get out.

"What the hell! Who are you? Get me out of here. I am really stuck," says Burton with panic in his voice.

His breathing is strained, and getting a good breath is getting harder and harder.

Lyndsey says to Nelson, "Let's go back to the boat and see if we can find any help."

"No, no, don't leave me. One of you stay here," pleads Burton.

Nelson says in a hard voice, "Sorry, man, but I think you were about to molest my cousin, Lyndsey, and I really don't appreciate that. I think you are where you are supposed to be. You have been in charge too long, and the girls have suffered. Now it's your turn to suffer. And you will suffer, believe me. So, bye for now, and we will send help, but I think we will wait until tomorrow."

Burton Douglas is in panic mode. He has spent all his professional life by the ocean. He never expected to die on the rocks above the ocean. Not now, not today. He is paralyzed with fear. He yells, but he is too far from the group in the cove below. Maybe Jan might hear him . . . but the ocean waves cancel his voice.

Lyndsey says, "Come on, Nelson. There'll be room for you in the boat now. I'll grab Jan on the way back and tell her I lost Burton."

"Okay, I'm just going to rearrange the rocks," says Nelson. He piles rocks around Burton's head so that he can no longer be seen, just heard faintly. "That should do it."

They leave a struggling Burton behind, who is now too tight in his rock grave to shout loudly. They grab Jan, who is still dutifully taking field notes.

"Hey, Jan. This guy needs a ride in the boat. Reckon Burton will be all right with that?" Lyndsey says.

"I guess," says Jan. "Weren't you with Burton?"

"He went off to look for some little critter. I didn't want to break my leg on those rocks. He said he'd meet us at the boat in ten minutes."

They all return to the cove. They wait for Burton, and they wait. But the light is fading, and the boat's skipper says they must return or risk being stranded. He calls the coast guard, who will send out a team by air to search. But they won't see Burton under his pile of rocks. Everyone, including Nelson, boards the boat and travels back to the school.

Burton Douglas has eight miserable hours to live.

Trapped, he knows he is in serious trouble. His body is cold and damp. The dark envelops him. He thinks he hears a rescue team, a helicopter overhead, but he knows they won't see him. They will send out a ground team at first light . . . if only he can stay alive till then. But a pain in his chest and down his arm tells him he won't be alive the next morning. He talks to his mother, who died years earlier, and he cries and repents. Too late.

Both Lyndsey and Nelson sense the moment of Burton's passing as an exploding firework in their souls. They know Burton Douglas is gone. Their dark passengers are pleased.

†

CHAPTER 22

THE FAMILY IS EXPANDING. Sabrina is the head of the family that possesses the gift. Her daughter, Lyndsey, is now married to Ernie Jones, and they have two children, Rob and Mary. Ernie, like Jason, has the gift from another bloodline, and Lyndsey and Ernie keep a close eye on their children. Is there a red swirl around them? No, not yet, but the chance they have the gift is greater with both parents possessing it.

Tiffany Rose, Sabrina's daughter, is now married to Manny Cruz, and they have one child, Lori. Tiffany has the family gift, but in a different form. She wonders, *Will Lori inherit this special family gift too?* An evil ancestor never means their descendants will all share their traits, but the twisted gene may skip several generations and show up as a red aura in people who have no idea of their genealogy, of their connection to evil.

Nelson is now married to Rita. He chose to marry her because he saw red in her and wanted to share himself fully with the woman he loved and keep no secrets. Her family, too, has the gift. They have two children: Robert and Jacob. Robert has not inherited the family gift, but Jacob has.

A total of thirteen family members with the gift.

Sabrina looks at the family and says, "I need to repeat this for our new family members with our family gift as a destiny for our growing family. We were meant to do this; we were chosen and given this special gift to rid the world of people not worthy of life, not worthy of existing. A true gift. The red that we have and we see allows us the strength, ability, and moral right to eliminate people.

"George Francis was the first in our family to try and understand the gift. He struggled because he was alone but added structure to our family. His son, Frank James, my brother and Kari's father, came next and better understood our position and added rules and further structure to the family. These two pioneers have led us to where we are today. We are expanding the understanding of the forces we are up against. Our main mission continues.

"It is important to stress that we must not get caught. We must murder to satisfy the inner monsters, the demons, and the dark passenger we all possess. We must not leave DNA, a road map right back to this family. If one of us gets caught, we all get caught. Discretion is important. We must also look out for each other. Help when help is required. We must act as a team. We must not go to jail. We are not made for jail. We must always have a member of our family in the justice system, such as an attorney or law enforcement. We must stay on top of the latest laws and look for neon red people that need to be eliminated. It is our job to keep the world balanced.

"We now know that there are other bloodlines doing our same work. We must team up with them when we can. We also know that the inner monster can be quiet for a long time, perhaps a lifetime, but once awoken, the inner monster will do whatever it needs to keep us alive. What we do is important. We are a *family*."

Each of the family members nods to Sabrina, indicating that they understand and are committed to the family as a team.

Sabrina then brings the family back to the current moment. "What calls for our attention now?"

Rita says, "We have a situation that requires our skills. I have been following a nurse at Kensington Hospital. Her patients are dying at a faster rate than any other nurse's. I have an inside source that suspects her of killing her patients."

Kari is shocked to hear this. Most of the family are treated at Kensington Hospital and have long been supporters of the hospital. Sabrina says, "Yes, this is important. Lyndsey, would you be able to help Rita on this?"

"Absolutely," says Lyndsey.

Morgan Ann Miller, a registered nurse, has been a long-term employee of Kensington Hospital, and, until lately, her record has been exemplary. But recently, patients have been dying in higher-than-normal numbers during her shifts in the emergency room. Rita, who is working temporarily in the records department, has been watching Morgan during her shifts. Morgan is five feet six inches tall with short, rich brown hair and a ready smile for everyone she meets, and her personality is perfect for a high-stress job. She is friendly and professional: a wonderful combination for an emergency room, where chaos is normal. She seems to be a good, dedicated, and professional nurse. So why such a high death rate in her care? Something is wrong. Something does not add up.

While Rita concentrates on her investigation of Morgan, Lyndsey begins to watch the other nurses on the same shift. Marie Jean Phillips and Matt Ryan Dalton are professionals and have been working in the medical field for many years. Marie is a heavyset professional with a mop of dirty blond hair in a messy bun on the top of her head. Adorable. Marie is her own person and has both arms tattooed in a colorful show of independence. The tattoos are beautiful, and all the patients comment on how much they like her ink. It is a good way to start a conversation, and everyone loves Marie as a nurse. Matt is a bit rigid, a stickler for rules, and he uses formal ways to treat a patient. He is thin but muscular with dark hair, never out of place, and a new mustache that makes him look like a cheesy TV detective from the eighties. Matt laughs at that, especially when they begin calling him M-Dog. Matt is younger than the other two nurses and, earlier in life, was on his way to a professional baseball career. Bad luck and a bad ankle break changed his trajectory in life. Baseball was over. He studied and worked hard and has become a dedicated registered nurse.

This emergency room team of three nurses becomes known as the M Squad. Morgan, Marie, and Matt. They seem to be a great team, but whichever shift Morgan takes, the death rate increases. Rita sees the statistics, but they do not make sense. Looking closely at her patients and the recorded treatment, everything looks in order. How could this be? An increase in deaths despite the administration of proper treatment from Morgan? It does not add up.

They all like being part of the M Squad. They think of themselves as minor superheroes and wear a small patch on their right sleeve that says *M Squad* in gold letters on a blue background.

Rita is stumped. So, she begins to dig deeper. The patients have nothing in common. Not age, sex, race, or type of injury. Nothing binds them together but death, it seems. Surely *something* binds them together. Even a little bit. While she is trying to find a common thread, Lyndsey searches in another direction. She looks at the employee records, hours, vacation, and sick days. Morgan has switched shifts three times in the last year. Why? Lyndsey discovers a trend. Matt switches shifts, and Morgan and Marie follow suit. To keep the M Squad together?

Lyndsey needs to talk to Rita. Something has fallen into place.

"Rita, I have been looking hard into these three. I found that they change shifts as a unit. We suspected Morgan was the killer, but I think we are wrong," says Lyndsey.

Rita nods. "I think so too. I have been looking at prescriptions and drug use during their shifts. I found something that looks innocent on the outside but is dangerous in the wrong hands."

"Tell me more," says Lyndsey, intrigued.

Rita says, "Matt has been taking eye drops out of the drug and prescription locker. Too many eye drops. Now, eye drops seem innocent, but the active ingredient is tetrahydrozoline. If this drug is administered to a patient in a shot overdose, they can die. The drug is not searched for and is hard to detect. Doctors are unaware of this type of death. It is never even looked for in an autopsy. The patient dies, and nobody knows why. The perfect crime?"

Lyndsey says, "I have also found a link to Matt. Many of the people who are dying have an athletic background. I think Matt is killing off the patients as a kind of bitter revenge for the fact he isn't able to compete anymore. Pure envy. Even if they are too old or not even currently in sports, Matt wants to hurt anyone in athletics because he was eliminated from an athletic career."

Rita says, "I think Morgan suspects. She may not be sure what he is doing, but she knows he's doing something. She reported Matt to a detective, who contacted our family to get involved."

Rita and Lyndsey contact Kari, who calls the detective and tells him the whole story.

Matt is called into the hospital security office. He has a pretty good idea why he is being called in. He is ready. Matt sits down across from the police officer. Rita, Kari, her detective, Lyndsey, Marie, and Morgan are in the next room, listening to the interview.

Matt says, "I hope this is to give me a raise."

No one smiles. Then the detective lays out what they suspect: that Matt has been killing patients with eye drop medication. A simple medication people use every day. Eye drops. Amazing and unbelievable.

Matt sits with his head down for several minutes. Then he looks up, furious. Lyndsey, Kari, and Rita all see how red he is as he says, "I admit that I have been overmedicating athletic patients with tetrahydrozoline, the ingredient in eye drops. I hate that I do it, but I also hate that I work in medicine rather than spend my days on a baseball field with fans cheering for me. Why should these people enjoy what I can't have?" Matt yells, then breaks down and sobs uncontrollably.

Suddenly Matt pulls two needles full of his eye drop medication from his clinical coat pocket and puts both into his knee and pushes the fluid into his body. Everyone is caught off guard. They rush to stop him, but it's too late. Matt smiles at them all, then his facial features collapse, and his body goes limp. Matt sinks to the floor. The room is quiet. Stunned silence. Matt is beyond help. In his mind, Matt is playing baseball and is up at bat with a full count of three balls and two strikes. The crowd cheers, the cheers fade, then Matt is no more. Another suicide. It is not what they were expecting, but their inner monsters are pleased.

Weeks later, Rita and Lyndsey are talking to Morgan and Marie when their new replacement nurse is brought in. "Everyone, this is Maxine, who will be working with you in the emergency room." Morgan and Marie shake Maxine's hand, welcoming her. They give her a gold and blue patch to put on her right sleeve. Morgan, Marie, and Maxine.

The M Squad lives on.

Maxine has beautiful tattoos on both arms. And green hair.

CHAPTER 23

SABRINA HAS BAD NEWS that she has only shared with Kari. She has pancreatic cancer. She first noticed weight loss, then her back hurt more than any time in her life. She went to the doctor and, after many tests, was told the awful news. Life-changing news. She is dying, and she knows she is dying. She decides to keep this information quiet for now but trusts Kari with the news.

For the last few years, Sabrina has been researching narco-submarines and how the drug cartels use these efficient methods of transporting large quantities of drugs into the United States. They are almost never caught because the submarines are built by cartels and use materials not easily picked up by radar. After her in-depth research, Sabrina wrote her first nonfiction book, *Under the Blue: The Story of a Drug-Running Narco-Submarine.* This book took Sabrina two years working undercover for a Mexican cartel with the support of the CIA and Drug Enforcement Agency. She learned the workings of a narco-submarine and how advanced the submarines were. Unfortunately, her book catches the wrong kind of attention.

The interest comes from a group known as the Iron Cartel, headed by a man who is descended from Joseph Stalin, going by an altered surname of Statin, and their goal is to take over the government of Russia in a violent coup. They want to go back in time and restore the former Union of Soviet Socialist Republics. They, along with many in Russia, revere Stalin and long for a return to Soviet greatness.

Ivan Statin contacts Sabrina for her expertise. In his experience, everyone can be bought, and he's sure he can offer her enough money to assist him. He arranges a call with her on the dark web, where their conversation cannot be intercepted. Sabrina asks the family to research him, and they discover his link to Stalin. Curious and determined to make a kill of great significance before she dies, she agrees to meet Ivan.

On the call, he says, "The Statin family has been following you closely and sees you as someone that can make our dream of dominance in Russia come true. We have purchased a narco-submarine with the capability to take a crew of twenty along with more than four tons of finished cocaine worth more than enough money to fund our coup."

He offers Sabrina an eye-watering sum to advise on the submarine mission. Sabrina agrees. The money will support her family when she's gone. But she insists that she be one of the crew. She knows her family won't like it one bit, but she doesn't want them to see her decline and her illness take her from them before their eyes. Ivan is surprised but agrees. Her knowledge of the submarine technology will be useful. And her offer to join such a dangerous mission makes him trust her more.

Ivan says, "We have other Iron Cartel members, not family bloodline members, planted in Russia to complete the task. Time is growing short, and the takeover of Russia is to take place on Victory Day, the day Russia celebrates its triumph over Nazi Germany in World War II. The day with much celebrating and parades is a day the Russian government will be distracted."

Sabrina replies, "The narco-submarine can get you to Russia unnoticed, but you will need to go long distances under the surface of the water. Riding on the surface only in the dark of night. As you get close to Russia, you will need to remain deep under the surface."

"The cartel's idea is to take a submarine to prevent suspicion. Planes, trains, and roads are too dangerous, and the chance of being discovered is too high. The Iron Cartel has decided that a submarine is the perfect way to get men and drugs into the country without being discovered."

With the date of their departure quickly approaching, Sabrina calls an emergency meeting of the family in her office. The ocean out the windows keeps up its rhythmic dance of waves. Always coming in, always moving forward. It is a sunny day, and the family is seated in the office, casually talking to one another. They are aware Sabrina is watching them all. Something is up. Sabrina looks tense. Something is wrong.

Sabrina looks each family member in the eye. She is a strong woman but is now vulnerable in front of them. She looks at her daughters, Lyndsey and Tiffany, a moment longer. They know something is up. They tense up for their mom's announcement. Sabrina says, "You know that I have been ill and can see I am underweight. But it is worse than I have told you. In fact, I am dying. I have pancreatic cancer that will kill me very soon. I am at stage four, and I can feel my time is short. I know this is a shock to you as it was to me, but these are the cards I have been dealt."

Sabrina's announcement is startling. Brutal. The room is silent. Not a whisper, not a breath. No one can believe what they are hearing. Sabrina, their leader, will soon be gone. Unthinkable. Unbelievable. The mood in the room has darkened.

Kari knows of this battle Sabrina has been fighting but does not give away that Sabrina has confided in her. She lowers her head and fights back tears. Lyndsey and Tiffany are open-mouthed with their hands on their hearts.

"How can this be?" says Lyndsey. "You can't leave us; we won't know what to do without you. Your knowledge and guidance are critical to the family, to us."

With tears flowing freely down their faces, they cannot speak further.

Everyone is crushed by the news.

Sabrina says in a strong, firm voice, "I am sick, and I am going to die, and soon. I am sorry I kept this from you, but I have a mission I have been working on so that I can go out with a bang and leave a lasting legacy. Something important. Something I must do. I am joining a submarine crew that is going to Russia to overthrow the government. I plan to sabotage their mission. It will be a fitting death for me. I pray I live long enough to complete the destruction of the submarine. I will set charges in the engine room of the submarine, and I need to be there to set them off. Should I feel the grip of death on me, I will activate the charges. They are small so as not to be detected, and they do not have the power to destroy the submarine, but they have the power to disable it long enough to bring about the deaths of all the crew."

The family is silent, but they are used to hearing about death. Just not their own. They are absorbing this news and dealing with it. Sabrina is dealing with it the best. She is a strong leader, a strong person. The inner monsters in the room are awakened and confused. Death is being discussed, but everyone is sad.

Sabrina says to the family, "I have decided that Kari will take over my role and move into this house and lead the family."

Kari responds, "It will be my honor to follow your lead. You have been an inspiration to us all. You are strong in the face of death, determined that the family continues. You will be missed more than I can say."

All the family circle Sabrina and place their right hand on her head as a sign of respect, love, and safe travels from this world to the next. The family is sad. Sabrina has been such a good and strong leader. To be without her is such a hard thing to comprehend. Each family member deals with the news in their own way.

Before she departs, Sabrina spends all the time she can with Lyndsey and Tiffany. They come to understand why their mom kept the bad news from them and why she was protecting them. They love her, and she loves them. It is devastating, but life stops for no one.

The day comes, and Sabrina says all her goodbyes. All the tears have been shed, and all the hugs have been given. The family leadership has transferred to Kari. Kari is now living in the house with the family office. With a last strong embrace from each family member and a prayer for success, Sabrina is off on her last mission.

Sabrina is seated next to Ivan Statin, and the submarine is traveling to its rendezvous with Russia and its fate. The submarine seems to function well, even though it is a tight fit and very uncomfortable inside and full of loud men laughing and joking.

Sabrina says to Ivan, "I hope your men are ready for what is to come."

"They are noisy but brave and determined men. When the time comes, they will be ready," says Ivan.

The trip is uneventful, and the submarine is traveling well below the surface. The time is close at hand, and the men can feel the weight of destiny. They are ready for battle and to take over the Russian government. As the submarine enters the Barents Sea, she goes as deep as she can, down to two thousand feet below the surface, in the Bear Island Trench.

Ivan congratulates Alexei and Dimitri Statin. "Well done, boys. You have done an admirable job at the helm. Everything is falling into place. The coup is underway." Ivan looks at Sabrina and nods his approval.

The trip has taken ten days, and the Iron Cartel are all claustrophobic, cramped, and exhausted, anxious to be out of this floating coffin and enthusiastic for the coup to begin. Sabrina is weak but maintaining a look of determination. She doesn't believe any of the crew have guessed her condition. Now that the time is near, she grows somewhat anxious too. She knows the submarine is getting close to the spot where it will begin rising to the surface. Within four hours, the submarine will surface, and the men will get out into the sweet, fresh air, and the war the men in the submarine thirst for will begin. Everything is in place. Sabrina knows she is in the start of the death grip that will soon squeeze the life out of her. She struggles to concentrate. She must fulfill her task or die in vain. She must stop this invasion.

For a moment she thinks back to her life, the eliminations she has participated in, the thrills and the agonies of her life, the proud moments with her family. Then, calmer now, she takes a small controller out of her bag and pushes a button, setting off a slow chain reaction. She has done what she wanted; the submarine will soon slow down and die. The same as her. She feels the thrill of death around her. She is excited that her mission will be complete, and she is also thrilled by the prospect of her own death. Such a strange feeling, wanting to live but also excited to die. She will soon experience what every human before her has experienced throughout history: annihilation.

Thirty minutes later, a small explosion goes off in the engine room. It is heard only by the crew member nearby. He radios the captain. The sub has stopped its forward momentum, and it now falls slowly and lands with a thump on the Barents Sea floor, far from the surface, far from fresh air and life.

Everyone looks to Ivan Statin for leadership and a way to fix whatever is wrong. Ivan looks worried and goes to Sabrina. "What happened? Why are we not moving? And what can you do to fix this?"

Sabrina feigns an expression of worry. "I have no idea what happened. Did we hit something?"

Ivan looks at Alexei and Dmitri for an answer. They shake their heads.

Ivan gives a hard look to Sabrina. "Did you do something to harm this ship?"

Sabrina is close to death but forces herself to say in a strong voice, "Now, why would I do that? I'm literally in the same boat you're in. If you don't get out, I don't get out. Why would I sacrifice myself?"

The submarine is quiet. No sound from the engine. The men are concerned but not yet panicking. Not yet. Sabrina's inner monster and dark passenger know they are about to die with their host, but they give her the strength to see this last mission through.

Ivan looks at the crew, mostly family, and wonders if any of them did something. Ivan then looks at the cocaine and the millions of dollars to overthrow the government and has a horrible thought. *What if we can't get out of here? No one knows where we are. The people on the surface waiting for us won't know something is wrong for two more days. And what could they do to save us anyway?*

Suddenly, the entire submarine goes dark; the lights are out, and the ventilation system moans to a stop. The men now are paralyzed with fear. Ivan is alarmed and fearful. The backup systems do not come on. Cell phones were not allowed on the mission for fear of being tracked. They are now missed.

The entire Iron Cartel has twelve hours to live.

The men sit in the dark submarine. With the ventilation off and the heating system down, the sub is getting colder and colder. Each man is alone in his own thoughts, even though twenty comrades surround him. Hour by hour, each of them becomes resigned to his fate. Hopeless, despondent, and broken. They must each face the fate that they know is coming. Oxygen is getting precious.

The pancreatic cancer has done its job, and Sabrina has done her job. Sabrina thinks of her family, her life, and her books. She has had a remarkable life, but now she is at the end. The end we must all face. Sabrina closes her eyes for the last time; she thinks of her father, Frank, and all the adventures they have had in this strange life they have lived, guardians of the world, eliminating those who threaten others. A strange life for sure. An exciting life. Will she be rewarded with heaven, or has she set herself up for hell? Do either exist? She is about to find out. Her breathing begins to go shallow. She can hear what is around her but in a dreamlike state. She cannot understand any more. She is between worlds. Then, without fanfare, she silently crosses over. She is no longer of this world. To Ivan and the crew, it will appear she succumbed to the lack of oxygen.

Ivan is struggling to breathe and keep out the cold. He can't figure out what went wrong. How did the submarine fail them? He listens to the moans of his men, his family. They are all dying a slow, agonizing death together. He looks at Sabrina, already gone. He knows his time is through. His dreams are dead, his men are dead, and soon he will be dead. He thinks of all the planning he did, all the connections he made, all the money he collected, and all the drugs he has on this ship. He thinks of all his family has sacrificed to get to this point. There is no rescue, no savior to help them. No hope. These are the last thoughts of a man who should be the leader of a great Russian country. The Statin family, militaristic blood relatives of Joseph Stalin, are gone.

But so is Sabrina.

The family is meeting in Sabrina's office, now Kari's office. The large windows still look out over the quiet, rolling ocean. The colorful artwork between the windows that Sabrina selected will remain. The corner cabinet that displays Sabrina's books is now also home to the awards that Kari has received during all her successful years as an attorney.

The family members are seated with one empty chair as an honor to Sabrina. Present are Kari, Lyndsey, Tiffany Rose, Ernie, Rob, Mary, Manny, Lori, Jason, Nelson, Rita, and Jacob, who all have the family gift. This is the largest number in the kill team that the family has ever had at one time.

Kari says, "We are all at a loss over Sabrina's passing. She died keeping peace and saving many from a bloodthirsty coup. A big feat, indeed. She is to be remembered as a strong leader who was dedicated to removing evil from our world."

Each family member knew what Sabrina was going to do, but the reality of what she went through is lost on them. The thought of a dark, cold sub, surrounded by dying men, slowly suffocating, excites their inner monsters, but their dark passengers feel the sadness of the loss of one of their own.

Everyone holds up a glass and salutes Sabrina as Kari says, "To Sabrina: our mother, our friend, our sister, wife, cousin, and leader. May she rest in peace and watch over us as we continue her mission to rid the world of unworthy, evil people."

They all drink to the past and the future. Silence momentarily overtakes the room; heads are bowed.

Then life must continue. It waits for no one.

Kari says, "In Sabrina's honor, let's discuss if anyone has something of interest to share."

"I do," says Nelson. "Rita and I have been following a person of interest. His name is Arthur Dillinger, and he runs a human trafficking ring that is growing. We think we can eliminate him and stop the entire group. We want to eliminate them before they grow bigger and more difficult to control. He acts as the leader, and there appears to be no second in command whenever Dillinger is absent. He is a brilliant red and needs to be eliminated. Rita and I would like to remove him from this earth."

The inner monsters in the room are on alert and desiring a kill. A thrill goes through the family members.

Rita says, "This ring often abducts young children for ransom. It is a surprisingly profitable business. It creates fear and emotional trauma for the family. The mental damage done to the children is awful. They feel stressed and afraid long after the kidnapping is over."

Kari says, "You have the family's blessing to go after Arthur Dillinger and his gang. Please be careful."

Their dark passengers are alive and excited. The room is abuzz with the thought of kills in the near future. The inner monsters are pleased.

CHAPTER 24

Nelson and Rita begin planning their capture of Arthur Dillinger by watching him carefully and noting his schedule. He meets with his team of six people each Wednesday afternoon. The six people, four men and two women, then begin to follow potential child victims. Nelson and Rita are trying to see a method and pattern to the kidnappings and are watching one evening when the team abducts two young teenage girls off the street. Nelson and Rita don't know who these girls are yet.

Emma says to Sophia, "That car is following us."

"Yes, I see it," says Sophia. "Let's walk faster."

They do, but two men jump from the car and grab both girls. They put up a fight but are overpowered. Emma is able to bite one of the men, but he hits her hard.

Sophia cries out, "Emma!"

"Shut up," says the man and punches Sophia.

Sophia's head is spinning, and she falls to the ground. The men tie them up, duct tape their mouths, and throw them into the car. The kidnappers are practiced and act too quickly for Nelson and Rita to react in time. All they can do is follow the kidnappers as they take the girls to a seedy part of town. Nelson and Rita stay back, watching as the girls are taken to a building and taken down several steps to a basement.

Inside, the girls are blindfolded and tied up with the tape still over their mouths. Emma is terrified but tries to communicate with Sophia through grunts. Both girls are shaken and trying to make sense of what is happening. The room smells damp and feels cold. The concrete floor they are lying on is rough and scratches their knees and arms. They try to sit up but are unable to. The blindfolds keep them in the dark.

Outside, Nelson looks at Rita and says, "Let's get them out of there."

They leave their car and approach the building, alert to anyone who might intercept them. They quietly descend the steps from the street and peer through a gap in the boards covering the windows. They can see one of the girls. They watch for several minutes to make sure the men are not still in the room. When they're satisfied the girls are alone, Nelson works the lock, which takes patience and a steady hand. Finally, he opens the door. The room has a wet concrete floor and is nasty, cold, and terrifying.

They reach the girls and whisper, "Don't be frightened. We are friends to rescue you."

As they are untying the girls, suddenly the interior door slams open, and Nelson and Rita are jumped and overpowered by the two men who kidnapped the girls. Nelson tries to fight back, but he is hit over the head with something solid and drops to the floor. Rita screams, and the men turn on her, and soon she is tied up too. The two men from the gang tie them up, blindfold them, and put tape over their mouths. They resecure the girls. Then they are all left on the cold concrete floor, battered and bruised. Two hostages are now four . . . but only the two girls are of value to the human trafficking ring. Nelson fears he and Rita will simply be killed.

For hours they are left alone. Nelson thinks, *There is no way out of here. Rita and I are in serious trouble, and these two young, innocent girls are in big trouble too.* All four are trying to get the duct tape off their mouths so they can talk to each other. Nelson has the most luck and is able to talk somewhat. "Rita, are you okay?"

Rita grunts, and Nelson takes that as a yes. Then he says, "Girls, I'm Nelson, and this is my wife, Rita. We watched you get taken off the streets tonight and followed you here, trying to rescue you. Grunt if you understand." Both girls try to make a noise. "Good. Okay, we are in trouble here and need to help each other when the opportunity presents itself."

Hours later they are cold, hungry, and miserable. Suddenly, Nelson smells a pleasant aroma with a distinctive vanilla scent. Someone has entered the room while they were all sleeping. Hands are turning him up to a sitting position, and his restraints are being removed. Nelson rubs his wrists and rubs his eyes to see what is happening. Rita and the girls are being freed also. Emma and Sophia start crying but seem to calm instantly when they see the man helping them. Emma says, "Thank you so much," before she and Sophia enter into a bear hug.

The man in front of them has a distinctive blue glow to him. A calmness, serenity, and peace fall over the room. He quickly ushers them all up the stairs and into a waiting van. Once in the warm van, they drive away from this dungeon. The man says, "I am Gabriel, and I was sent here to help you." He has a calming blue color and a pleasant aroma with a distinctive vanilla scent that follows him wherever he goes. They are safe. They are unafraid of this man.

The man takes the girls to each of their homes without asking for their addresses. He tells the parents to call the police and assures the parents the girls were not violated and this experience will quickly fade from their memories. Nelson hears this and believes this experience will quickly fade from all their thoughts. Long-term fear and emotional trauma will not follow them but will end here tonight. Nelson does not know how he knows this to be true.

Gabriel then drops off Nelson and Rita, but they are confused by this priestlike man who rescued them as he drives them to their house. Nelson says, "Who are you? How did you know we were in trouble? How did you know where to find us? And how do you know where everyone lives?"

Gabriel simply says, "What you need to know is that when you needed saving, I was summoned. All four of you are good people and deserve a right to live your lives."

Then Nelson says, "Gabriel, we were planning to go back and eliminate these bad men, including Arthur Dillinger."

Gabriel nods his head in approval as he drives away without answering any other questions. As they tend to their injuries and take showers, Nelson and Rita are lost in their own thoughts. The blue aura of the man is something they've never seen before, only a red aura. What could this mean? The rest of the family will need to be told.

They know they have had a lucky escape tonight. Without the blue man, they would be dead. This is a sobering realization. But there's a problem: Arthur Dillinger has not been dealt with. By now the gang will know they have lost their "product" and will be making plans to replace the girls. They will have to take action soon. They cannot, however, risk going back into the building. They will have to take this gang out from a distance. This is where their weekends at the gun club will come in handy; both are excellent marksmen.

So, still bruised from the day before, Nelson and Rita find a spot on top of the building opposite the gang's HQ and wait. And wait. And wait. From time to time, Nelson gets a whiff of vanilla, but whenever he looks around, he cannot see anyone but Rita.

Finally, a member of the gang emerges from the building. Rita has him in her sight and pulls the trigger. Right through the heart. Down he goes. The sound of gunfire brings a few more out of the building, and between Nelson and Rita, they get all but one. There's only a matter of minutes before the police are called. They need Arthur Dillinger.

A minute later, he appears at the door to the building. He looks in their direction, spotting them on the roof. He pulls his gun out and begins firing, but the gun is useless. It is not jammed but unable to function. Nelson smells a faint smell of vanilla. The man with the blue aura must be nearby helping them with their mission. Nelson points his gun at Arthur and pulls the trigger.

The inner monsters are elated. Filled with joy as Nelson and Rita leave the scene. As they are exiting, the police are entering. They soon surround the building and point their guns. All they will find are a few of the gang cowering inside the building, the rest dead outside.

Nelson is driving and buzzing with excitement. Rita is excited too. They pull over and take some deep breaths.

"Did you smell vanilla?" asks Rita. "It has to have been that man from yesterday. Did you see him?"

Nelson shakes his head. "I didn't see him, but I know he was there. His scent is his mark."

"Who is he?" Rita asks. "He was our guardian angel. He said we should call him Gabriel."

The next day an emergency meeting of the family is called.

Nelson and Rita discuss their night. Nelson says, "We thought we were saving the two girls, but then we were attacked, and all four of us were tied up and gagged. Without hope and without any way to get free, the impossible happened."

Rita continued, "A wonderful calming scent with just a hint of vanilla and a peaceful blue aura surrounded all of us. A man was standing in between us, freeing us from our bonds, protecting us, and transporting us from danger. He called himself Gabriel."

They tell the story of "Gabriel" and how he turned up, unseen, to help them take out the gang. The dark passengers and inner monsters are all abuzz with excitement, and electricity crackles throughout the room at the story of the killings.

Nelson says, "Who is *Gabriel*? And what is the calming blue light and intoxicating smell with a hint of vanilla?"

Kari has a thought, and when the room quiets down, she stands up and says, "Family, I think I know what the blue man with the delicious scent is. We have the red people who have committed serious crimes against humanity and need to be eliminated. We have semitransparent people who are bloodline relatives of evil men. Perhaps the blue-glow people are here to help us."

The room goes silent. Curious and cautious. Then the family begins to discuss the situation. Could there really be angels? The family has never thought of angels before, but perhaps they are a kind of angel, dark angels that carry out dark deeds but for the good of humanity. Could there be light angels too? People who protect the innocent and protect the dark angels? Unbelievable, but wonderful if it's true. After a lengthy discussion ensues and no real conclusion appears, the meeting adjourns. Kari sits to ponder the concept that angels might be looking over the family. It is a welcome sign that a higher power approves of their mission and is there to help when help is needed the most. She sits in her chair looking at the ocean. Thinking. Wondering.

After the meeting, Jason needs to let off some steam after the strange revelations, and he goes for a run. He likes to run, not only to manage stress but to keep fit. As a jet pilot, he sits a lot and knows he needs running to keep him fit for duty.

At the same time, Kelsea Robinson is taking her daily jog through the woods and along the stream. She runs almost every day and takes the same path, plugged into earphones and listening to Bruno Mars. That heavy beat is soothing to her. She runs to the music and is lost in her own world. Today, as she goes around the familiar right-hand turn in the coastal redwood forest, she is suddenly grabbed, and a gloved hand goes over her mouth. She is shocked out of her Bruno Mars world and into the reality that she is under the control of a stronger being who is wrestling her to the ground.

Kelsea, however, is not a little girl simply running; she is a force to be reckoned with. A high school track athlete and a champion at long distance, she has been training to join the elite track-and-field team at the University of Oregon. She will soon be running for the Ducks.

She tries to scream, but the hand over her mouth is too much, and she cannot get out a sound. She screams for help mentally and is fighting hard not to be subdued.

Jason is also running with headphones, playing his favorite training music, including "Eye of the Tiger," "The Final Countdown," and anything by Creedence Clearwater Revival. Suddenly, he hears a voice over his loud music. A distressed call for help. He stops, takes off his headset, and clearly hears a "HELP."

The voice directs him to a location not too far away. He runs toward the sound. The voice is getting louder and louder and more desperate. Suddenly, Jason comes upon a strong-looking man wrestling with a girl under a redwood tree on a jogging path.

Jason yells, "Hey! Stop!" as he makes a grab at the man holding this girl.

Jason is instantly in fight mode and tears at the attacker. But the man is quick and fights off both the girl and Jason. He punches Jason in the stomach hard, and Jason momentarily loses his breath. The man jumps up and runs to a hidden motorbike, jumps on, and is gone.

Jason is lying on the ground, trying to get his breath, when the girl reaches out and tries to help Jason. He pushes her hand away gently. "I'm okay, just pissed off that he was able to sucker punch me." He sits up, gathers himself, then stands up. He is concerned for the girl's condition.

"Thank goodness for your good timing," says the girl.

Jason holds out his hand. "I'm Jason, by the way."

"And I'm Kelsea," says the young girl with a solid handshake. She has dark eyes, long black hair in a ponytail, and an athletic build.

"It's amazing I heard you shouting for help. I have my music really loud," Jason says.

Kelsea smiles. "I didn't actually shout."

Jason frowns, confused. "I heard you pretty clearly. I know what I heard."

"Oh, you heard me," she says. "But I called for you telepathically. Shouting in the face of my attacker would have probably gotten me killed. I'm just glad you picked up on my communication. Very few can."

Jason says, "Wow. That's quite a skill. Did you know the man who attacked you?"

Before she can answer, Kari, Nelson, Tiffany, and Lyndsey all appear. Jason is shocked to see them. *This jog couldn't get any weirder*, he thinks.

Kari says, "What's going on? We clearly heard someone in trouble. We all heard it together and rushed over to help. Looks like Jason got here first."

Kelsea is shocked that four people heard her mental call for help. "Do you people all know each other?"

Jason laughs, "Kari is my wife, Nelson is my son, and Lyndsey and Tiffany are our cousins. We are family."

Kelsea is gathering herself and now wearing a sweatshirt from Kari to cover her torn clothes.

"Well, thank you for helping me. Is there anything I can do to repay you? And why are you all red?"

Jason, Kari, Nelson, Lyndsey, and Tiffany are all shocked. "You see us as red?" they ask.

"Yes, like you've all been sprayed around the edges with red paint," Kelsea says. "You guys are red, but that guy was nearly invisible. That's why he managed to grab me so easily. I hardly saw him coming."

This is incredible. Here is someone with not one power, but three!

Kelsea says, "This is not the first person I have seen that is almost invisible and certainly not the first red person I have seen."

The family members look at each other in disbelief.

Kari says, "Kelsea, do you have any thoughts that are unusual when you see these people? Do you have any deep thoughts that make you feel like an outcast or at least different from your friends?"

Kelsea says, "I have had these thoughts all my life that I want to harm someone. Someone that is red or almost invisible. My friends think I'm crazy, so I rarely talk about it. Are you saying you understand me?"

"Kelsea, we do. We are part of a family that has a gift of seeing evil people, who show up red. We do what we can to fight these evildoers in the world. Would you like to meet with us and discuss what we do and who we are? You seem like you would fit right in."

Tiffany Rose says, "I think our whole family would be very interested in your telepathic abilities."

Kelsea smiles. "Yes, I am in."

CHAPTER 25

AT THE NEXT FAMILY MEETING, Kelsea is introduced.

Kari introduces everyone to Kelsea. "We met her a few days ago in unusual circumstances. Kelsea is a track-and-field star at the local high school and is about to join the University of Oregon as a long-distance runner. She was practicing the other day and was abducted by a man waiting in the redwood forest she runs through during her training. He was waiting for her and would have surely raped her except Jason was nearby also running to stay in shape."

She concludes, "What made this unusual was that the man had his hand over Kelsea's mouth so she couldn't scream or call for help. But Jason heard her voice as if she *was* screaming for help. He ran to save her. Nelson, Tiffany Rose, Lyndsey, and I were not that far away and heard the same cry for help, so we went running in her direction. By the time we had gotten there, the man had run off."

Nelson says, "The important thing here is that Kelsea was able to communicate with us nonverbally. All four of us clearly heard Kelsea. She can also hear us telepathically communicating to her. Amazing, right?"

Everyone agrees and gives Kelsea a thorough questioning to find out her history with this special gift. At the end of the inquisition, Kelsea says, "Thank you for having me at your important and secret meeting.

After talking with Kari, Jason, and the others, I think I can be useful in your quest to rid the world of unworthy people. What you have felt from a young age I have also felt. I feel like I've landed in a place I was meant to be. I will be a junior member if you will have me. I will learn fast, and I feel I can contribute with my special ability. Very few people can communicate with me telepathically, but four members of your family have been able to. Maybe more. I would like to send out a message to all of you, and let's see who can hear me."

She sits down, and with her hands lightly on each side of her temple, she sends out this thought: *If you can hear me, put your left hand on your right shoulder.*

Kari, Lyndsey, Tiffany Rose, Jason, Nelson, Rita, and Jacob all hear Kelsea and respond with the gesture.

"We can all *hear* you, Kelsea," says Jacob.

But Ernie, Rob, Mary, Marie, and Lori cannot. Lori says, "Kelsea, we could not hear you."

Kari says, "Okay, so we know who can and who can't communicate telepathically with you. This will be important on future missions."

"Now, for everyone who can hear me, I want each of you to give me an instruction, telepathically," says Kelsea.

One by one, they silently tell Kelsea to put her finger on her nose, to make a sound like a horse, to lick her lips, and other things to show that the communication is real.

At the end of the test, Kari says aloud, "We are glad you are here. You are family to us."

Kelsea says, "Can I be part of the mission to find my attacker? I would like to see him off the streets."

"Kelsea, you had mentioned he was semitransparent, and Jason described him as red. This means he has evil in his family history and is actively evil himself. Jacob, I want you to work with Rita to track this guy. Jason needs to be involved because he has seen him, but Jason needs to be in the background. Jacob, he has not seen you or Rita, so you can get close to him without him knowing it. Rita, you can communicate with Kelsea when we have a definitive name and location." Kari then turns to Kelsea. "Kelsea, I need you to keep training along the same path as you always take. He may be looking for another chance to grab you. We will have you covered with other family members."

Doing research, the team finds out that the police are aware of a serial rapist but have no active leads. This man has been moving around the city with no pattern. It seems that now he is trying his luck along the redwood forest trail.

Rita, Jason, and Nelson are in the small town located on one end of the running trail. They are eating lunch in the outdoor area, watching people walk by. Some are glancing at storefronts, and some are casually meandering along the main street. A very pretty girl about eighteen years old goes by wearing a loose top and tight-fitting jeans. She is a stunner, and everybody takes a quick look as she passes by. About thirty feet behind her, Jason spots the man. He pulls his cap low and hides from view but lets Nelson know, "That's our guy."

Nelson gets up from the table and follows the man, who is fixated on the girl, when suddenly a well-built man greets her. "Hi, Holly," he says as he swings her around off the ground.

"How's my big guy, Javier?" she says, and they walk away hand in hand.

The target puts his hands in his pockets and walks away defeated. Nelson shadows him until he walks into Hidden Hills Apartments, unit 429. Nelson goes to the mailboxes and looks at 429 and sees the name Bobby Ray Kenny. He returns to the café, where Rita, Jason, and Nelson start to look him up. He is a distant relative of Billy Ray

Kenny, a serial rapist known as the North Hill Rapist, sentenced and put to death in 2004.

Bobby Ray Kenny is their man. After surveilling him for three days, they discover that he often goes into the redwood forest along the running trail, waiting and watching.

Nelson says, "I think he wants to get caught and be known as the Redwood Forest Rapist, like his ancestor."

Kelsea does her running each day, carrying a special something with her. A week later Bobby Ray Kenny is in the redwood forest waiting. Kelsea is running her trail and gets a telepathic message from Rita: *Bobby Ray is waiting in the redwood forest. We have eyes on him. Be careful. If he does attack you, we are here, and no harm will come to you.*

Kelsea is not worried about harm coming to her; she is concentrating on the harm she is about to do to Bobby Ray Kenny. Bobby will not be happy.

As she runs past a thick grove of Redwood trees, Bobby reaches out, but Kelsea swerves. She pulls a knife from her belt and turns to confront him. He is taken aback and stops in his tracks. They face off, each deciding who has the best odds of success. Kelsea's weapon gives her the upper hand. During this, Kelsea is telepathically calling for backup. But she wants her revenge. Kelsea lunges for him, keeping her weapon low. Bobby Ray Kenny howls and holds his bleeding groin, dropping to his knees in pain.

In less than a minute, the backup arrives. They keep Bobby Ray Kenny in his place on the ground, sobbing and crying out in pain until the police arrive. They take a statement from Kelsea as the ambulance arrives and take witness statements from everyone else, who tell the cops that the incident was clearly self-defense.

The police then take Kelsea to the hospital. Once she is cleared and released, she goes back to the family and thanks them all. Her family.

At the hospital, she is able to find out about Bobby Ray's condition. Kelsea's quick thinking and knife skills mean that Bobby Ray Kenny is no longer a threat to any woman. His days of pleasure at women's expense are over.

Although there is no death that day, the inner beasts and dark passengers are satisfied with the blood that has been spilled.

CHAPTER 26

MARIO MAYFIELD IS A WANTED MAN. *So what?* he thinks to himself. He has been wanted most of his life. Early on, it was petty theft, then assault, then later possession of drugs. But he has never been caught. Always wanted but never captured. He just moves out of an area once he has committed enough crimes that police start looking for him. An endless cycle of moving and committing crimes. This suits Mario just fine.

In each new town he gets a new girlfriend. Easy, with his devilishly good looks, bad-boy attitude, and money, which he has intermittently. Other people's money. But the girls love him, and he moves in with them in every town. Just when the girls start to get committed to him, he is gone. A new town, a new girlfriend, more crimes.

His luck stays with him right up until he moves into the town where the family lives. Only a few blocks away is Kari's home and the office where all the plans for people like Mario are hatched. The office where they are currently discussing the latest victim, Bobby Ray Kenny. Bobby is no longer a threat to Kelsea or any woman. Everyone in the meeting is happy justice has been done. An appropriate justice. Quick, severe, and final. No courtroom drama here. No defense team insisting, "He was framed; you got the wrong guy." And no need for a long sentence, not now he is harmless.

Other matters are discussed, but it keeps coming back to Bobby Ray. Even the inner monsters, the dark passengers, are excited. He may still be alive, but he has still lost his life. He has been neutered. They'll keep an eye on him, of course. A man that frustrated and angry could still be a danger to society, but they aren't worried yet.

"All right, everybody, it looks like we will not be getting any business done today. Enjoy the day, and we will see you all at the next scheduled meeting," Kari says, smiling.

As everyone is leaving, Lori stays behind to talk to her mom, Tiffany Rose. "Mom, for my eighteenth birthday I've decided I'd like to have a beach party with some friends with a cookout and a bonfire."

"That sounds great; let's make it happen," says Tiffany.

Lori goes down the staircase and out the front door. She walks right by Mario Mayfield perusing the neighborhood for opportunities. He is guessing which house might have money or items he could easily steal and sell, and he sees Lori coming out of her aunt's house. Lori is cute, with long brunette hair streaked with blond and brilliant-white teeth behind an infectious smile. Mario is instantly interested.

"Hey, gorgeous," he says, turning on the charm with a winning smile.

Lori blushes and walks on.

"Sorry. Didn't mean to be a jerk," says Mario, catching up to her. "It's just that you look friendly, so I wondered if you'd mind helping a stranger out."

Lori keeps walking; this man has a tinge of red, and she doesn't want to confront him alone. Best to play along and get out of harm's way. "Help out how?"

"I'm new in town. Trying to meet some people, settle in, you know?" he says.

"Sure."

"What do people do around here? Where should I hang out?" he asks.

Lori shrugs. "Depends what you're into, I guess. But you'll meet a lot of people at the beach."

"Of course. But I can't just go up to people, can I? It would look creepy."

"You're doing it now," Lori says, laughing.

"Oh, you're a smart one," he says. "But you know what I mean."

This is a man her family might be interested in, so Lori decides to take a chance.

"I'm having a beach party next week," says Lori. "I don't know why I told you that, but I guess it makes me happy, so I just blurted it out."

Mario's face lights up. He thinks his plan to ensnare Lori is working. Little does he realize, it's Lori's trap. "Thank you, I would love to come to your party," he says.

Lori blushes again under his gaze. "Next Friday, four o'clock at Irish Rose Beach."

"It's a date," says Mario. "What's your name? Mine's Mario."

Lori smiles and says, "I'm Lori."

"Well, little Lori. I'll be seein' ya." With that, he turns at the next street while Lori continues on her way. At the first opportunity, she'll fill her mom in on Mario.

During the next five days, there is a rash of burglaries and petty theft. Kari's house is broken into, but Kari and Jason have a sophisticated security system that screams at Mario as he breaks a window to gain access. He runs like the wind, but a camera has caught a picture of him running away. A clear picture.

Mario is concerned, but the beach party is only two days away, and he is looking forward to seeing Lori again (although he knows she's too young to be interested in him), but perhaps he'll be able to lift a few wallets with his light fingers. The party will have a lot of rich folk there. If nothing else, there will be food and fun.

For the next two days, Mario is constantly stealing this and that, selling to the next town's pawn shop. He gets some money but never very much. A couple of hundred dollars gets him a motel room for the night, food, and some to spend on any girl within his sphere. He is striking out with the girls, but that is all right. Tomorrow is Friday, and he has a party to go to at the Irish Rose Beach.

Friday arrives. Lori is excited to party with her friends, who are all laughing, throwing footballs, wading in the ocean, and standing around a bonfire, some dangling marshmallows over the flames. A barbeque is smelling delicious to one side. Mario approaches Lori and says, "Hey, Lori, nice party. I'm so glad you invited me."

Lori blushes and says, "Well, you kind of invited yourself. But you're welcome. We have chicken and steaks and a lot of side dishes. Pepsi, Sprite, and water. These are all friends and good people. Enjoy."

Lori has briefed her family about Mario and that he has a hint of red but nothing too alarming. He probably isn't dangerous but he must be, in some way, a "bad'un," in her words. The family watch for her signal that Mario has arrived.

Mario looks over and sees six adults enjoying the party, but off to the side so as not to interfere with Lori's friends. There's Kari and Jason, Lyndsey and her husband, Ernie, and Tiffany Rose and her husband, Manny. They are having food, drink, and conversation while the teens are having a blast with each other. A successful party. When Mario arrives, Lori gives them a big wave. This is the signal. Jason looks at Mario and instantly recognizes him from the security footage.

Jason is on full alert and tells the other parents.

Mario loiters around the fire. Most of the partygoers are wearing bathing suits and beachwear, but he's in jeans and a T-shirt. He casually surveys the party area, guessing where all the valuables are: a safe place close to the parents. He eyeballs the treasures and thinks, *Easy-peasy, all that is mine. Just got to be careful.* The kids would be easy to fool, but parents are a bit more difficult. But this is not Mario's first rodeo.

Jason is on to Mario. He calls Lori over and suggests that she introduces Mario to all her friends.

"Hey, Mario, come here. I want you to meet my family and friends," says Lori.

He trots over and shakes the parents' hands. They all think him very charming. Then Lori takes him over to her friends.

While Mario is distracted by Lori and all her friends, Jason and the dads take all the money, credit cards, and driver's licenses out of the wallets and purses, noting what each wallet or purse contained so that later they can put these items back. Then they put the empty wallets and purses back. Then the parents take a walk along the beach, leaving all the valuables alone, while Jason hides behind a bench not far from the loot.

Mario realizes the booty is unattended and excuses himself from Lori's friends, who are all too childish for him. When they are all huddled around the barbeque, helping themselves to the burgers, he slips away. He casually walks over to the pile of valuables and quickly takes the wallets and purses, stuffing them into one of the beach bags. Without looking back, he walks quickly away, heading to the dunes. Watched, of course, by Jason.

In a secluded spot, among some trees, Mario stops. His curiosity about his haul is too strong. But, to his surprise, there are no money or credit cards. *What the hell?* Then, to his bigger surprise, Jason appears from behind a tree and grabs Mario red-handed.

"Hey, man! Get off me!" Mario yells, but Jason has a firm hand on Mario.

Mario fights back, but Jason is holding him tightly. Ernie and Manny rush back, and the three have Mario captured.

"You tried to steal from these kids," Ernie says.

"And I know you're a thief," Jason adds.

"This was the first time, man. Just let me go. No harm done. I only needed some money for my rent," Mario says, trying to sound sincere.

"This is not the first time. I have information from the pawn shop owner in the next city who identified you from the photo my security system took of you trying to rob my house," says Jason in a level tone.

Mario withers in the hands of his capturers; he is finally caught and knows he is going to pay.

The family could have dealt him a quick, decisive punishment, but Mario is still young and has a whole life before him. The family at the beach party decide to let the courts deal with him. His red aura is not nearly strong enough for more serious retribution, and they know he has a chance to turn his life around. But someone has to put a stop to his thievery.

Before the police arrive, Jason says, "Mario, you are young. Decide how you want to end up. We will put in a good word for you with law enforcement, and you might not end up in prison. But if you come into our sights again and you have not redeemed yourself, we will make a different decision about your future. Your short future."

Mario knows he can't escape or talk his way out of this situation. Finally, after all the crimes, he has been caught. That reality shocks him into thinking about his life. The police come, take a report, and take Mario away in the back of a police cruiser. He watches the kids enjoying their lives and living freely and envies them as they drive him away.

At the next family meeting, Kari says, "Mario Mayfield has been charged with a variety of crimes and will spend the next year in prison on multiple charges. We, as a family, decided it was better for the police to deal with him. He was a wispy red and can be saved if he wants to. Jason gave him a stern talk, and hopefully he will listen. We do not give second chances often.

"We have compassion when the crime calls for it, but our mission is to eliminate those who do mental or physical damage to others. Then we have no compassion."

Kari walks toward the large glass windows looking out at the rolling ocean waves. She is thinking of the family and the great strides they have made in eliminating the undeserving. The red people who are guilty of murder or mental abuse, the semitransparent representing the potential for evil, and now the blue, angelic people with a wonderful scent with a hint of vanilla—angels. The family has been on a long road from the days of George Francis and Frank James.

She turns toward the family and extended family. "I am proud of each and every one of you. Our forebears, George Francis and Frank James, are watching over us and are proud of our progress and devotion to our mission. I want to offer my blessing to you all. We need to be careful out there and not get distracted. Please keep a single focus when out on a mission."

Kari looks at each person in the room, one at a time, and nods her approval of them. They in return nod back, accepting and returning her approval.

"Any people of interest we need to be watching closely?"

Mary stands up. "I have been hearing rumors in our school about our math teacher and football coach, who gives out drugs to the football team. It is an uncomfortable situation because he seems like a nice guy, and the students relate to him. He is a young teacher, and the students like that. But there seems to be a dark undertone. His name is Dominick Amaral."

Kari listens carefully. "Mary, see what more you can find out about him and see if you can get any of the football players to talk. Jacob, I want you to ask your buddies at school if they are familiar with this Mr. Amaral. Nelson, I want you to find out what he does outside of school hours—what he does and where he goes and what his habits are. Anyone else have a concern?"

Manny stands up and says, "There is a new freight service delivering packages that I'm concerned about. It's called Danny's Freight Line. There has been talk that they are using the freight lines for human trafficking and drug distribution. They need to be looked at."

Kari said, "Manny, you look into their operation but be cautious, discreet. Ernie, you work with Manny and see what you can find out about their deliveries and distribution and who leads this operation." Kari then says, "This meeting is adjourned." Then she adds, "Everyone be careful."

Mary starts asking other students at school if they are having any problems with Mr. Amaral, the math teacher and coach. Almost everyone says no. But two guys say that they were meeting Mr. Amaral after class during his office hours in the room where he meets students on a one-on-one basis to talk about his class assignments and to discuss grades.

Robert says he met with Mr. Amaral to see if he could get his math test grade up. He says that Mr. Amaral said he could raise his test score if he tried drugs that Mr. Amaral was selling. So, he did, and his test scores got better. He told his friend, Jake, who was also having math problems. Jake went to Mr. Amaral, and the same thing happened: he locked the door, offered Jake coke, and charged him for the drugs, and his test scores improved.

These are the only two guys who admit what they have done with the teacher. There are probably others. Meanwhile, Jacob finds out that, as a football coach, Amaral has closed sessions with his receivers, quarterback, and running backs just before the games and at halftime. The word is that Coach Nick, as he is called, is giving cocaine to these players to have a better performance from them. It is a secret that all the players know but do not discuss. The coach charges the players and swears them to silence. They win more games than ever before, and they enjoy the glory. Winning is a drug too, and Amaral exploits their competitiveness for his own gain.

Nelson researches the teacher's off hours and discovers that he frequents many clubs in the area known to be owned and operated by the so-called DanDan Jamaican Cartel. This is where he gets his cocaine. He often visits the Cat Club, enjoying the ladies trafficked by the DanDan Cartel. Illegal and often underage. The girls are promised work in the modeling business, but most of the girls know that will never happen. A dream promised but never fulfilled.

Marie and Ernie are investigating the DanDan Cartel and find them to be a ruthless gang led by a narcissistic and malicious man with a large scar along his right cheek from a past knife fight. His name is Marley Brown. His crew are ruthless and dominate the drug business in the area by eliminating the competition. The women and girls who are trafficked are just another source of income for the cartel.

When the family members get back together, the consensus is that Dominick Amaral and Marley Brown have a connection. Dominick is dealing drugs to many of his football players. The DanDan Cartel is dangerous, and both the drug and human trafficking must be halted. The family members talk and devise a plan to halt both Dominick Amaral and the DanDan Cartel. A devious plan.

CHAPTER 27

ADIO AZAN RULES THE DRUG TRADE and all human trafficking in Jamaican territories. He is respected and feared even by all the cartels and his government. Adio is very unhappy to know that the DanDan Cartel has decided to expand their small Jamaican business to the United States. Marley Brown did not seek his permission to expand and did not let Adio Azan, nor any of his men, know that this move was taking place. And to paint his trucks the colors of the Jamaican flag was an insult.

To be human trafficking also—capturing and kidnapping young girls from Jamaica to bring to America to be sex workers—is more than Adio Azan can tolerate. Marley Brown and his cartel show no respect to Adio by presenting him with profits from their endeavor. This is not to be tolerated either.

But Marley Brown *has* been sending profits to Adio Azan every month. Large profits to show his respect, like he is required to do. But Manny and Ernie from the family have a mole in Marley Brown's gang and intercept all the money before it reaches Jamaica. They know this will cause a rift between Adio and Marley.

They are right. Adio is furious.

Ernie and Manny also let the Jamaican leader know that the girls being kidnapped from Jamaica are being disrespected and beaten in

America by Marley. Adio is boiling over and needs to teach Marley respect and use him and his cartel to make an example so that others will not even think of disrespecting Adio.

He sends word to Marley that he and all his cartel are to meet Adio on a large ship in the bay. The meeting is to be top secret. Adio wants Marley to think that he's impressed and wants to meet one-to-one to discuss the success Marley is having. Marley feels special and honored to have Adio Azan, the top dog, meeting him personally. Marley tells Dominick Amaral he is to accompany him on this trip so that Adio can hear about what's been happening from the horse's mouth. Marley has no idea what is about to happen.

The family has a lot to do with setting these two men on a collision course. Marley has been sending a generous portion of his profits to Adio every month, but Adio has not received a penny. He is about to teach Marley a lesson in respect.

The night of the meeting, Marley is dressed in his best outfit befitting a king of a cartel. Marley knows he is about to be honored for his hard work by Adio, and he has acquired some girls for the party to follow. Dominick Amaral is excited to be a part of this historic meeting and wears a black suit with a crisp white shirt, an open collar, and no tie.

On board the ship, the members of Adio and Marley's gangs wait for Adio to arrive by helicopter. Drinks are served, and the girls are below deck. Finally, a helicopter is heard getting nearer. Anticipation is growing. The helicopter lands, and Adio Azan emerges in a leather jacket that seems to sparkle. He is bigger than life.

Two large bodyguards surround Adio but let him move freely among the DanDan cartel members. Marley holds out his hand in a gesture of gratitude to shake Adio's large meaty hand. The two embrace and share a drink together.

"Your men are all here?" asks Adio.

"Yes, sir. I am a little nervous not having some of my men at the club and watching our drug trade, but per your request, we are all here. I have the girls resting below, and I want to introduce you to Mr. Dominick Amaral, the coach with a great football record."

"So, you are the one plying your football players with cocaine before football games?" asks Adio.

"Yes, sir, and I give them more at halftime. I also give some to my students wanting a better grade in math. Life is good," says Dominick with pride. Dominick is proud of his accomplishments. But suddenly two of Adio's men grab Dominick roughly and hold him tight while Adio looks at him with dead eyes. Dominick is alarmed and fears for his life.

Adio says sternly, "You put our cartel in jeopardy by selling drugs to your football team members. Cocaine and strenuous football is a deadly combination. Some kid will die, and then the authorities will be looking for where they got drugs. You have been foolish to sell drugs at a school. You jeopardize my business and my livelihood."

Dominick is now alarmed. He is hopeless in the tight grip of the bodyguards. Adio pulls out his glock and shoots Dominick right between the eyes. In a nanosecond, Dominick goes from being a proud drug dealer to a dead one.

Dominick's body falls to the floor. Everyone else then takes out their guns, all ready for action.

Adio says, "Put your guns away. This man had no integrity. There are plenty of people who want our drugs; we do not have to put young lives on the line. I have my limits, and this man has exceeded them. Let this be a lesson for you all: if you offend me, I will shoot you. Take him away and dump him overboard with an anchor. I do not want to hear about him again."

Marley is shocked and confused, thinking, *Since when do we have rules about who uses our drugs?* But he is not about to question Adio and risk offending him.

Adio says to Marley, "Come with me to the captain's quarters. My men have brought white rum for your men. Enough to kill the devil, as we say in Jamaica."

While the men stay on deck to drink the white rum and toast the night, over and over, Adio and Marley go to the captain's quarters and sit facing each other. Adio says to Marley after giving him a large glass of white rum, "You go to America and expand your cartel without my permission. You run a brothel, stealing some of the most beautiful women in Jamaica, again without discussing this with me. And yet no money from your expansion makes its way to my hand?"

Marley protests, "I send you my cut every single month. I have never missed a payment. What are you talking about?"

"I receive nothing from you. Ever."

"Why would I come here knowing that I'd not paid my dues? That would be suicide! I swear I have wired the money!" Marley is trying to figure out where all that money went. "Someone on my crew is betraying me."

Adio frowns. "If you are being screwed over, clearly you are incapable of running your operation. I cannot have incompetent people in my outfit."

"Give me a few days to figure out who is responsible. I will hand them over to you to do with them what you will," Marley says, his heart racing.

"Too late, I'm afraid. As we sit here, your men have drunk a sedative, and they will all be passed out for the next twelve hours. Your men will be traveling to Cuba to be picked up by the Cuban government. You, however, will not make it to Cuba. You are about to be tied to an anchor and thrown overboard."

Marley screams at Adio, "I did send you money every month. I sent a lot of money. Do not kill me. You are making a mistake."

Adio ignores Marley and tells the captain to head straight to Cuba. A plane will be waiting there to fly him back and out of danger with the Cuban government. Adio tells the captain to dump Marley in the ocean in two hours. Marley whimpers, knowing his fate is sealed.

Adio gets on his helicopter with his two bodyguards, one the mole, and flies off.

The news reports the events: "Authorities boarded a large vessel off the coast of Cuba early this morning for a routine check. A Cuban official announced that they apprehended a number of men, reportedly from a Jamaican cartel, who were found aboard in a sedated state. It is believed that the men were sent to Cuba deliberately as an act of gangland retribution, since the members of the cartel are wanted in Cuba for human trafficking offenses."

There is no mention of Marley. Nobody knows he was aboard the vessel and that his body is at the bottom of the ocean, food for the many tropical fish. Neither is there mention of Dominick Amaral. Nobody would guess that a teacher would have been aboard this vessel. He is reported missing by his family, but they have no idea where to begin looking for him. Like Marley, he is also fish food. The boys on the football team celebrate his absence, and the next football coach gets good performances from them without drugs.

On hearing the report, the family is abuzz. They don't know what happened to Marley or Dominick either, but from the electricity that runs through their veins, they know the two men are dead. The inner beasts, the dark passengers, are pleased.

At the next meeting of the family, everyone congratulates each other on the destruction of Marley Brown, the DanDan Cartel, now withering in jails in Cuba, but especially the death of Dominick Amaral, the schoolteacher that drugged teenage athletes. All gone or put away for life.

Such a wave of electricity runs through the family meeting. The inner beasts are satisfied and swimming in death. But the mission to provide justice is not over. Much work lies ahead. The world is full of undeserving, red people. But Kari is a force to be reckoned with, and her family is a deadly tool, and they act as one.

"Going after cartels is a good strategy for our family. We get to kill many evil birds with one stone. Our next target is already known, but this cartel doesn't deal in drugs. There is a cartel whose prime mission is to strip the world of its sand to be used in construction. The world is growing, and more housing is needed. More housing means more infrastructure, and it all means more concrete. A main ingredient in concrete is sand. Sand trafficking is a huge problem. It seems to be a mundane resource, but it becomes an environmental issue. The impacts are substantial. Coastal ecosystems are ravaged. Vegetation, soil, seabeds, and marine life are disturbed and often cannot recover. Such destruction of the environment is a danger to all humanity, and I believe their actions will cause much suffering."

She explains that they'll be going to focus on a major player in this sand harvesting, the Sand Storm Company. They illegally tear riverbeds apart and sell the sand to the highest bidder. The family's job will be to disrupt the workings of the Sand Storm Company. The main man of the company is Anant Sharma, a mean-tempered man. He is ruthless to his men and feared. His second in command is Raj Bakshi, a much more likable, coolheaded man. He has a softer side and is a counterbalance to Anant.

Kari says, "Nelson, we will need your pilot services. Lyndsey, track their locations. Ernie, you'll be on the ground where they are working. And Kelsea, you'll be there too. You will be able to communicate with us telepathically. The family will offer support, but you are the team assigned to tackle this assignment."

Nelson is the pilot of the Bombardier Learjet 35A. Lyndsey, Ernie, and Kelsea are in the cabin of the jet going over the details of their mission. Their destination is Colombia, one of the most ecologically diverse countries on Earth. Sand Storm has large container ships that carry great quantities of sand from one location to another on the world's oceans. These great ships are largely automated. No need for many crew members to ship sand from one port to another. Nelson and Ernie are the logical choice of family members to sabotage these ships, and they know how they are going to do it. Lyndsey and Kelsea are going to be on the ground in the areas of digging to disrupt the sand trafficking as much as possible. They are working up an email they are about to send to Anant Sharma, which will thrill him and then destroy him.

When the jet lands, Nelson and Ernie leave in a truck loaded with the equipment that they need to do their part in destroying the Sand Storm Company. They drive down to the shipyard and locate the six ships specifically designed to transport unpackaged bulk cargo. In this case, sand. These are not double-hulled ships because a small leak would not cause an environmental catastrophe like an oil spill would. The Sand Storm operates single-hulled with only a skeleton crew for security. They also have limited personal computers monitoring the ships. Load them up, send them out, unload, and return. A simple but very lucrative trip.

Lyndsey and Kelsea leave the jet center and drive their Range Rover to a spot overlooking the river being torn apart without any consideration for the environment or marine life. They take out a computer and intercept a message. They have been intercepting messages going back and forth for months.

> **Anant Sharma, the Sand Storm Company.**
> Dear Mr. Sharma, per our recent correspondence, I wish to conclude our discussion with a twenty-million-dollar gold transfer to your account for eighteen bulk shiploads of sand. This will be for three complete trips for the six ships you operate. Per our agreement, after the delivery and acceptance of one ship, the funds will be transferred in full.

Anant licks his lips. The biggest sale of his life. He has turned down everyone else to get this contract from the Thorson Construction Company, a mafia-run construction company delivering some of the world's most celebrated construction projects. They are serious people and not to be played with. Everything must run absolutely smoothly to continue this contract and for future contracts. Anant Sharma calls his second in command and yells over the phone, "Raj, get those ships moving. I know he will pay after one ship, but I want them all loaded and shipped. I want to impress them with our efficiency. Now get those *damn* ships moving."

Lyndsey and Kelsea are excited that the email did its job so well. At the same time they were intercepting messages to Anant, they were also intercepting messages to Harald Thorson, the mafia chief of the Thorson Construction Company with projects all over the world. Lyndsey and Kelsea's adjusted emails assure Harald Thorson that the eighteen shiploads of sand are being sent to him for a total of only five million dollars in gold, not the twenty Anant expects. This is sure to cause a big problem when the first shipment of sand arrives.

Before the great quantities of sand arrive, Ernie and Nelson board the first ship to leave the port, posing as marine mechanics, and lay explosive charges every forty feet along the keel. The small security crew has no reason to doubt them. They are there to protect the valuable cargo; they are not trained marine mechanics. The faked identification and certification documents that they look at seem legitimate, so Ernie and Nelson gain easy access to place the timed explosives in the engine room.

Kelsea has done her job. She has been to the Colombian sites where all the workers are digging up the sand beds and loading large trucks with the cargo, posing as a surveyor. She plants a number of human skulls in the dry riverbed downstream from the workers. Then a few more a bit further down. She telepathically communicates to Lyndsey, *All skulls are in the riverbed where the workers are about to begin harvesting the sand.*

Lyndsey communicates to Kelsea, *Come back to the Range Rover. The fun is about to start.* According to local folklore, these skulls are a bad omen. They know the workers will quit digging immediately and will not return to the area. Kelsea and Lyndsey are sitting in the car when they hear a commotion. The workers are running away from the riverbed. All machinery stops, and everyone is running away from the site. Never to return. The plan worked like a dream. The Sand Storm Company, knowing nothing (and caring less) about local culture and tradition, would never have expected this.

Raj Bakshi doesn't have enough sand for the whole shipment. He is able to load only one ship for now. But he understands that the entire payment will be made on the arrival of the first ship. He has some time to bring in other workers, ones with fewer superstitions, he hopes. He calls Anant and tells him, "Boss, we had a little trouble at the river site, but we can talk about that later. I'm reporting that the first ship has left port and is on its way to the client."

But Anant should be worried.

Not another grain of sand will be taken from this riverbed. The Sand Storm Company will never find another person in the country to work on this cursed property: Lyndsey will make sure of that. A viral campaign she launches on TikTok draws attention to the exploitation of the land, and a group of committed activists sets up camp at every one of the Sand Storm Company's sites, which slows sand extraction to near zero. But that comes later.

Back to the voyage of the first ship. Two hours into the automated trip, as the ship is in deep water, there are muffled explosions. It draws the attention of the security crew, who discover there are fires in the engine room. They valiantly try to extinguish them but aren't paid enough to risk their lives. They disembark the ship in a lifeboat and get as far from the ship as they can, fearing a massive explosion. No sand will reach the Thorson Construction Company.

Lyndsey and Kelsea monitor the emails going back and forth between Sand Storm and Thorson. The intercepted emails are now in explosive territory. There is confusion, with the Sand Storm Company demanding their twenty million in gold, but the Thorson Company is angry about never receiving any sand and insisting the amount is five million dollars.

Soon, Harald Thorson's men are at the doorstep of the Sand Strom Company. They have come to greet Anant Sharma and Raj Bakshi with their guns drawn. In a brief but deadly hail of gunfire, Anant and Raj are no more. Without its CEO and facing a stock crash and public outcry at their destruction of ecosystems, the Sand Storm Company goes quickly into administration. But the damage has also been done to the Thorson Company, which has no sand for its construction projects.

Angry investors pull their finance from the stalled projects, and no other agency is willing to trust Thorson again after his illegal trading practices. In a few months, his business fails too.

The inner beasts are pleased not only with the deaths of Anant and Raj but also with the deaths of these companies that pillage the earth of its precious resources and threaten life in these valuable ecosystems.

CHAPTER 28

THE FAMILY IS FEELING GREAT that they have had some impact on the illegal sand trade in the world. They shut down the Sand Storm Company and Thorson Construction Company. The holes in the boat's hull redistributed the stolen sand from the rivers to the ocean. The sunken ships will create a habitat for marine life too. On top of that, a couple of unscrupulous men are dead. It's an outcome the family can be proud of.

The family is pleased with themselves. But they should not have taken credit for the success so early. Little do they know that they are now squarely in the sights of Thorson, who is furious about the sand debacle.

Harald Thorson is not a man to cheat, and he feels he has been cheated out of his lucrative business. He is angry about having to rebuild an empire at his age. He has lost everything he cared about, and his children will not inherit the business.

Harald reviews Sand Storm's security footage of the sand harvesting operation. After trawling through hours of footage, he notices a girl walking the banks of the river prior to the workers. There are no women on these sites, so who is this girl? He puts his best private investigators on it. A week later, they report back. The site manager did not know who she was. A widening of the search reveals CCTV recordings of the same girl with three other people at a restaurant in the nearest town to the site. They are seen walking into a hotel, and the hotel records provide them with names. No flight manifests from commercial airlines that have their names on them, so they must have flown privately. The investigators follow this lead and discover a Bombardier Learjet 35A was logged at the airport about the time all the trouble started. They find the flight plan files with this jet and review the route, destination, estimated departure, and estimated time of arrival. All the information they need to find out who these people are has cost Harald so much money and time.

Their identities now known, Harald is hell-bent on revenge. This family of Americans will be sorry they messed with him. Harald wants them to pay. To pay with their lives. Harald Thorson needs the world to know you do not hurt Harald Thorson and live. He must make an example of this group. Without the family's knowledge, they are targeted for death.

Harald sends out a crew of seven men to find this family and eliminate them. And to do it in a most public way, so as to discourage others from thinking they can cheat Harald Thorson. A public execution, a show of strength, an example that death is the price of cheating Harald.

The family is unaware that a contract has been taken out on them. They sit securely in their office, warm in their seats, happy and content. They should be on alert, but they are not. However, equally unprepared are the men who have been dispatched to kill the family. They are not aware that one of the family has picked up signals of their arrival. As they get closer, Kelsea picks up an alarm.

Kelsea suddenly sits straight up in her chair with a loud moan. Everyone in the family looks at her in concern. "We are under attack," she says. "I can hear men talking about us; I can hear them think about our family. They are on their way here to do us harm. To kill us, to eliminate us. They are sent from Harald Thorson."

First everyone is stunned but quickly is on full alert. The family, with Kari as their leader, jumps into action.

Kari sternly says in a loud, strong voice, "The first thing we must do is leave here and have the Thorson men meet us in a more favorable location, one in which we can control the confrontation. The second thing is to capture Harald Thorson. We can fight small groups, but he will send wave after wave of men to kill us. We must capture him when he least expects it. Which is now."

She points to Nelson. "Nelson, prepare the jet and take the family to a remote island with few residents and tourists. We will have the upper hand there if we prepare. What island might that be?"

Nelson thinks for a moment. "I think one of the Polynesian islands. Let's say Easter Island."

Looking at Ernie, Kari says, "I need you to hack into Thorson's device and let him know we are headed to Easter Island."

Looking at Jacob, Kari says, "Jacob, I want you and Kelsea to go to Harald Thorson. Think of a way to capture him. Jason can then bring you all to Easter Island."

Nelson says, "We'll take him to Isla Salas y Gómez, a boat ride from Easter Island. It is a small, uninhabited island: a good place to threaten a mafia boss."

Everything is set in motion. Bad guys are coming; good guys are preparing. The family spreads out in multiple directions.

The war is about to start.

†

CHAPTER 29

THE FAMILY ARE LOCATED ON THE ISLAND, preparing for seven heavily armed men to come for them. Harald Thorson has declared war on the family, a war he fully intends to win.

While his men are heading to Easter Island, Jacob and Kelsea, in disguise to avoid being recognized by Thorson, are tracking an unsuspecting Harald Thorson. Her task is to find Harald and telepathically communicate with Jacob and to capture him using Kelsea's mind and influence.

The stage is set, and in two different locations, the war begins.

Seven men in camouflage are quietly sneaking up on a cabin on a cliff and facing the mighty Pacific Ocean. The full moon cannot be helped. This is the day and the time the family is to be eliminated. Harald Thorson has demanded that those responsible for cheating him from his money and business be killed as a show of strength. The men are spread out and approaching the house from six directions. They have wireless radios to communicate with each other. They all hear, "Men, check in. Number 1 here, all set; Number 2 here, all set; Number 3 here, all set; Number 4 here, all set; Number 5 here, all set; Number 6 here, all set."

They creep forward. They cannot see each other. Surprise is their mission. They are fifty yards away from the cabin. Shadows are seen on the drapes. There is action in the house; smoke coils up from the chimney.

The men hear, "Check in. Number 1 here, all set; Number 3 here, all set; Number 4 here, all set; Number 5 here, all set; Number 6 here, all set."

"Number 2, come in. Number 2 report."

Number 2 is silent.

They continue to creep forward. "Check in. Number 1 here, all set; Number 4 here, all set; Number 5 here, all set; Number 6 here, all set."

"Number 2 check in, Number 3 check in."

Silence.

They are fifteen feet from the house. "Everyone get ready. Full loads, fire when I tell you. Kill them all. No mercy."

As he is saying this, Number 4 is close to Nelson. Nelson does not move an inch. Number 4 has not seen him. As Number 4 edges past Nelson, Nelson pulls a Buck knife silently from his belt. A bead of sweat drips down the right side of his face. He quickly grips Number 4's face and slashes his throat while holding his mouth. Number 4 slides to the ground without a muffled sound. Nelson moves on, looking for Number 5. Quietly he scans the terrain and spots a man in the shadows. But he sees Nelson and aims the gun in his direction. Nelson quickly throws his Buck knife, and the knife goes into Number 5's eye. Nelson is quickly on him, covering his mouth and pushing the knife deeper into his eye. Number 5 is dead.

"Check in. Number 1 here, all set; Number 6 here, all set."

"Where the hell are you 2, 3, 4, and 5?"

Silence.

"Okay, on my order, rush the house and fire. Three, two, one, GO, GO, GO."

There is firing, but from the house, not into the house. Number 1 and Number 6 are quickly gunned down, dead. The leader is severely hurt and dying. Nelson lifts his head and says, "Why were you sent to kill us? Who else is coming? What can we expect?"

The leader says in his last gasp before dying, "You are all dead; you just don't know it yet." All seven are dead surrounding the house.

The family is safe. For now.

A long way away, Kelsea has identified Harald at home, in his study, waiting for his men to report that all is done, that the family is dead. The call is not coming. The call will never come. He is distracted by the doorbell. But his guard is at the door. Maybe the guard locked himself out, the idiot. He does not want to leave his phone because he is expecting his important phone call at any minute. But the doorbell rings again.

"Goddammit," he mutters. He begrudgingly leaves his office chair and walks down the staircase. He goes to his front door and finds it open.

"Dennis?" he calls. But the guard is nowhere to be seen.

He is nervous now. And he doesn't want to be outside in the biting cold. He steps out of the door and looks around. *This isn't right,* he thinks. But before he can retreat into the house, Jason appears from nowhere, and Jason smashes him hard in the face. Harald has been hit hard before and lashes back at Jason. Kelsea has the vial at the ready, but Harald swipes her away with a powerful hand. Jason hits Harald hard again, and, just for a second, Harald hesitates. In that instant, Kelsea succeeds in pushing the needle into the back of his neck. Harald collapses. He is immobilized. He can see, think, and feel, but his body will not respond to his wishes. He can't talk. *What the hell is going on? Let go of me,* he tries to say, but language is not available to him.

Jason and Kelsea take a moment to recover from the fight before they secure Thorson in the car and drive him to the nearby airstrip where Jason's jet is waiting.

Within six hours, Thorson is sitting on a rock pile on Isla Salas y Gómez in the middle of the Pacific Ocean, staring at Kari. The effects of the brownish liquid have dissipated. He is heavily and tightly tied up and can hardly breathe.

"Comfy there, Mr. Thorson? I hope not. We are here to talk, but I will be doing all the talking. If you think you are going to live, if you think you are going to get out of this situation, you had better give me the answers I want. Not what you are thinking but what I am thinking. Your life depends on it."

Thorson, groggy, tries to focus on Kari.

She continues, "First, your seven-man kill squad is all dead. Second, you are on very thin life support yourself. You came after my family. That is a death sentence in my mind, but I am going to give you one chance to keep your life. Do you promise to let this vendetta go and allow our family to be left alone? Do you promise to buy sand that does not upset the ecology? And do you promise not to use illegal sand harvesting for your projects?"

Harald says gruffly, "When I get out of here, I am going to shred your family, with you the first to die, slowly and in front of your entire family."

"Wrong answer," says Kari. "You are not the only tough one on this small island. You have met your match in me."

He growls at her and says, "Do you know who I am? What I can do to you? What I will do to you?"

Kari says, "Do you know who I am and what I am going to do to you right now?" She pulls a three-foot sword from its sheath. "Any last words?"

He spits at her.

She draws back and, with a mighty swing, slices into him deeply. A fatal swing. He screams for a few seconds; he knows he is dead.

Harald Thorson, with an anchor tied on him, heads toward the bottom of the ocean.

The inner monster and the dark passenger are impressed with the savagery shown by Kari when her family is threatened.

The family all heads home from the harrowing adventure. Kari has left Harald Thorson in the Pacific Ocean off the coast of Isla Salas y Gómez, never to be seen again. The ride home for everyone is a pleasant ride. An enemy who was dedicated to killing them off is no longer a threat. The head of the Thorson Construction Company is no more. The family is safe.

They are tired from the encounter but elated from the deaths that occurred. The inner monsters and dark passengers are alive and electric. To stare death in the face and win is very exciting. The entire family participated. Teamwork is wonderful when no harm comes to the family.

Back home in the family office, Kari starts, "Thank you one and all. We were tested. We were tracked. We were tagged for death, but we stood up, we stood firm, and we were victorious. Be pleased with yourselves. Our mission to rid the world of the undeserving is a continuous journey. One we must not let up on. We must stay vigilant. We can take this afternoon to pat ourselves on the back and put praise on each other, but after this afternoon, we are back to task."

CHAPTER 30

KARI IS SITTING IN THE SUN IN HER OFFICE, looking out at the ocean and the constantly rolling waves and reflecting on the path the family has taken since George Francis first began the family. She is warm and content as she contemplates his original need and desire to kill just one person, to feel what it was like to watch the life drain out of someone, to watch the breathing accelerate then slow and finally stop, to watch the eyes fill with terror at the knowledge they were about to die, to sense the soul leaving the body.

George Francis trained his entire life to experience this sensation. He selected a person he felt was unworthy of life. This began the family's goal to rid the world of the unworthy: those that have murdered or caused mental damage to another.

She remembers how Frank James carried on the lifestyle. George had been so shocked and distressed at the news his son had the same need as him that he had a heart attack. But when he had come to terms with it, George managed to work with his son and teach him the lessons of taking a life, which became the basis of the rules the family now kills by.

The family grew, and after Frank James's leadership, Sabrina took control of the family members with the gift. Sabrina was a leader who encouraged a team approach, and the family became a kill team. She led and added rules and guidelines to keep them safe. The family began to be a force and began making a mark on the world by eliminating those that choose to live a life without morals, without rules, without conscience. Sabrina showed the family what full commitment was when she sacrificed herself on her final mission.

Along the way, Jason had come into the family, marrying Kari, and was discovered to have the gift even though he was not a blood relative to the family. Lyndsey then showed the family that the inner beast could come out of nowhere to protect you. Next, Tiffany Rose brought her insight and ability to spot potential evil. Then Kelsea brought telepathic communication to the team skill set. Finally, most astonishing of all, the family had discovered the existence of people who appeared blue, not red: guardian angels protecting the vulnerable. The family has come a long way and is now a steady force, committed to protecting the world the best way they know how. Kari wonders about all the adventures and eliminations that will be in the family's future, how the kill team might expand even further, and what dangers they will face.

Kari sits in her warm office, comfortable and watching the waves out the window. *All is good,* she thinks.

Little does she know that the future she is about to face is uncertain.

THE END

ACKNOWLEDGMENTS

I want to thank the following people for listening to my story and adding important comments. It is a journey to write a book, and I always enjoy friends on my travels.

Thanks to ***Jenny Rose***, my wife, for listening and allowing me so much time in my study to write. When inspiration hits, you have to be ready to devote time to your craft. Often the inspiration will hit in the middle of the night. Writers will understand this.

Thanks, ***Javier Lopez***, my son-in-law and coauthor on *When the Day Ends...and Dreams Begin...* books one, two, and three, children's stories and poems for bedtime and the classroom. Thanks to Javier and his wife, my daughter, Holly, for encouraging me along this exciting journey.

Thanks to my children who make my life better: Krista, Holly, Joel, and Madison, who is always with me.

A special thanks to Gillian Barth, production editor, for her support, hard work, and ability to always get back to me quickly. It is appreciated. And thanks to Mascot Books and Amplify Publishing Group.

ABOUT THE AUTHOR

DON ROSE is a United States Army veteran and a graduate of the University of California, Berkeley. He is an artist, author, and retired landscape architect. Don lives in the Sierra Nevada mountains with his wife, Jenny, and their wonderful dogs, Uncle Frank and Miss Betty.

Guilty and Free: A Novel is Don's ninth novel and the second in the Dark Passenger series. Other books written by Don Rose in collaboration with Javier Lopez include:

When the Day Ends . . . and Dreams Begin . . .
When the Day Ends . . . and Dreams Begin . . . 2
When the Day Ends . . . and Dreams Begin . . . 3

Other books written by Don Rose include:
AMAZING Adventures of Young SuperHeroes
Mornings with Uncle Frank
Afternoons with Miss Betty

Another book written by Don Rose and Frank Southers is *Puppy Dog Tales.*